HUNGRY KYA?

FUEL 4 ENTREPRENEURS

SEEMA SINGH BHADORIA

Popular Prakashan
www.popularprakashan.com

Published by
Harsha Bhatkal for
POPULAR PRAKASHAN PVT. LTD.
301, Mahalaxmi Chambers
22, Bhulabhai Desai Road
Mumbai - 400 026

First Published 2020

(4528)
ISBN: 978-81-7991-994-1

Cover Design: Jai Wadhwani
Layout: Anjali Sawant

PRINTED IN INDIA
by Rashmi Graphics
#3, Amrutwel CHS Ltd.
Ganesh Galli, Lalbaug
Mumbai - 400 012

Contents

BON APETTIT!

PREFACE

The other day, a friend of mine called me for some advice. She talked about how she had spent many years working in the IT sector and was now looking at starting her own venture. She wanted my inputs on what she should do. She shared two or three ideas that she had been toying with, and asked me which one would be the best bet to ensure a successful business, one that would propel her into the big league of noteworthy business entrepreneurs. Our conversation set me thinking, about what really is a secure way to go ahead with starting a business on one's own and ensuring it does well. Is there really a fool-proof mechanism to work on an idea and create a business that will grow steadily, perform well and ultimately expand into an empire?

I started looking back at all the great organisations I had come across in the twenty-two odd years of my professional experience. I tried to examine the myriad factors that made these organisations tick. Slowly, I began preparing a draft in my mind of how one could build a great business model that would ensure that a company continued to grow exponentially and deliver profits, year on year. I analysed the different aspects involved—the break-even period, the investment priorities and focus areas, the risks one takes along the way...The questions seemed endless, but my rational mind worked back and forth to clearly see a pattern in all the companies which consistently did well. Then I started looking at how many of those things I had practised in my previous organisational role. I realised that therein lay the key to success.

In the 22 years of experience I had amassed, in diverse roles across industries, I was fortunate to have gained exposure to multiple fields of work. I had the opportunity to learn from all these varied experiences; every industry I had worked for had taught me something new. My seven-year stint in telecom, which started in direct sales, required me to understand TRAI regulations and IT technology, while my wide-ranging interpersonal interactions taught me how to deal with different kinds of people and thereby improved my emotional intelligence. Handling marketing for the branch offered the chance to work closely with advertising agencies; getting trained and subsequently training others opened up a new world of learning; bringing innovation to telecom by tying up with media houses for value-added services helped me understand how a business needs to diversify in order to survive; creating customised helplines, working in tandem with software development teams, paved the way for yet another sphere of business expansion. My four-year stint in the multi-level marketing industry was fertile learning ground, lending new meaning to my understanding of how a market can be created for any product so long as the foundation is firm and there is an aggressive approach towards introducing the product in the market with constant research to bring in freshness and innovation. Working with the serviced offices business gave me valuable insight into the workings of the real estate industry, teaching me about how the profitability of a business could be altered if the real estate angle was evaluated properly. I saw retail businesses perish as well as boom based on the real estate options they chose. Working with a media house taught me about marketing plans, introducing me to the fundamental concept of branding, about what did and did not work for different brands, and the constantly changing face of media employed to catch consumer attention. My last role as business head, then COO, and subsequently CEO, gave me a wonderful overview of how the creation of the right organisational culture could bring different-minded people together to deliver. One of the biggest learning lessons in handling business there came from understanding how finances need to be managed efficiently in a tight cash flow situation to keep things rolling.

On my way home from work that day, I kept going over in my mind the intricate pattern of assorted elements that create a successful business venture. And that is how the idea for this book was born. A book that I feel sure will foster the journey onward for many start-ups, that will help many young people learn what it takes, as exposure to new things and lessons taken from the experience of others before us is the one sure-fire way to keep learning and successfully create something new on one's own.

Speaking of entrepreneurship…What is it that drives people to passionately follow their dreams? For it takes great courage to live one's dream. I have had the chance to meet a lot of people who struck out on their own for a variety of reasons and purposes—some left rosy careers to live their dreams, others did so for family reasons. Some wanted to be their own boss, while some others thought they could create much more on their own… The motivations may vary, but only those who work passionately and persistently to take their dreams forward go on to create magic.

Take the example of Steve Jobs. He displayed entrepreneurial abilities at a very young age. He spent his early days with his father in the garage, taking apart cars and putting them back together. It is here that he learnt the value of attention to detail from his father. He was passionate about everything he did. For his school summer project, at age 12, he called Bill Hewlett, founder of Hewlett Packard, to ask for some computer parts. Hewlett was so impressed that he offered the young boy a summer internship. Jobs was not interested in formal education and decided to drop out of college. He learned calligraphy for a while, and it was this stint with calligraphy classes to which he attributed the iconic creative style that Apple is sought after for. He even decided to embark on a seven-month trip to India, travelling using local transport in UP, Delhi, among other places, imbibing a spiritual education that transformed him into a Buddhist.

By age 20, Steve Jobs had tied up with a school friend, Steve Wozniak, to redefine computers and technology. They started with a 'blue box', a digital technology device which could be used to make long distance calls for free. Its success laid the foundation for the Steve duo working further to create the first prototype of the Apple machine. There was tremendous labour and persistence on their part to get things moving, and soon their undying labour started producing the results they wished for, as they began selling gadgets that everyone loved. Steve Jobs led a frugal life in his father's garage, meeting clients and working laboriously.

Realising the interest his products were generating, he starting chasing investors until Intel agreed to fund him. He took Silicon Valley by storm and became one of the richest people in the country.

Soon, however, personal problems caused turbulence in his professional life, and at age 25, he was asked to leave Apple. Not to be deterred by all this, Jobs set up another company, NeXT. The machines were priced heavily, though, and he could not boost sales. Later, NeXT merged with Apple to create the first iOS (the mobile operating system used by Apple devices).

Aiming at building a bigger business empire, he ambitiously invested in a graphics company called Pixar which went on to make millions. NeXT and Pixar were bought over by Apple. The board of directors at Apple found that without Steve Jobs, things were not really going well, and they felt that there was no one more suited than him for the job at the helm. Jobs took over as CEO of the company. Apple grew by leaps and bounds under his leadership as the iOS made waves in the market. His perseverance to triumph against every professional and entrepreneurial debacle, to rise from the ashes every time he was faced with obstacles, is the reason why Steve Jobs built one of the biggest companies in the IT technology sector which continues, till date, to be an inspiration for the entire world. There is no shortcut to success, he proved. It can be achieved only by constant ideation, persistent effort, and a never-give-up attitude.

They say Thomas Alva Edison failed a thousand times before he got it right, but it was sheer persistence that ultimately paid off when he created the magical electric bulb. How many people would keep trying as he did, undaunted even after facing failure that many times? Yet, only such people who relentlessly persist in their pursuit are able to rise from the ashes like the phoenix. Edison lost money in many of his entrepreneurial projects, but he always bounced back and made up for all the losses incurred with whatever successes he achieved.

These stories are but testimony to the fact that nothing can let an entrepreneur down if he truly believes in his project and constantly strives towards achieving his goals without letting any hurdle, difficulty or disappointment deter him. The journey can definitely become easier, no doubt, if there is a path to guide him along the way, a path that has been tried and tested by others before him. This book attempts to present to its readers that knowledge which has helped many big businesses achieve success against all odds.

This book also is a token of dedication to my father, who forever possessed an entrepreneurial streak. Even though he served in the Armed Forces, he constantly endeavoured to live the entrepreneurial life by pushing his brother to start an enterprise. Many of these efforts failed, because even though he ensured the vision and finances were in place, the driving force was my uncle who lacked the same passion for the business. However, post-retirement, my father was able to fulfil his dream of creating something, when he started a school for the underprivileged to provide quality education to the children of his village. We may have lost his physical presence, but his dream certainly lives on.

Acknowledgements

This book is a culmination of the varied experience and exposure I gathered through my professional life of over 24 years along with life experiences spanning close to half a century. It is a reflection of the learnings I imbibed from professional leaders, peers, trainers, and all the wonderful people I worked with, that helped me understand wide-ranging aspects of success and failure in business and sharpened my outlook on creating a successful business module. My myriad experiences with customers were a great learning ground for how a business model could be refined and fine-tuned to better appeal to them. I have incorporated in this book many experiments that I undertook in my professional career to put forth teachings based on the results of these experiments.

I also attribute this book to my constant habit of observation, introspection and learning from people around me that gave me a better perspective on business and growth. I wish to thank entrepreneurs who made it big in life and whose stories I read to seek knowledge and inspiration, which have found mention in my book based on the information I have gathered and interpreted as per my understanding.

All specific mentions made in this book are purely for the purpose of learning and adding value to building successful businesses, and are in no way meant to cause any harm or damage.

The biggest thank you goes to my husband who has always stood by me. He provided me both inspiration and courage to go ahead and work on this book, and valuable feedback that allowed me to improve. I would also like to thank my mother-in-law who has often been a solid support in helping me balance personal life with work, letting me go all out to put in long hours at work, encouraging me to grow professionally. I want to thank my children who have become independent and accountable, taking off my shoulders a lot of the things that I needed to do as a mother; they have been extremely supportive.

I would like to thank my publisher Popular Prakashan for their enthusiasm to publish a book which looked at business from the lens of a woman and the editorial team which worked with me to make my writing erudite!

This book is dedicated to my father and mentor who always made me question my limits and wanted me to live life on a full canvas, where I kept working to add value to people's lives as well my own.

INTRODUCTION

The Evolution and Adaptation Process for Sustainable Business in 2020

With technological advancement and innovation in businesses, business models need to be adaptable for sustenance and growth. Businesses which understand this and reinvent themselves will continue to expand their horizons. In case of long-established, traditional businesses which are unable to adapt to the changing business environment, if they do not innovate, they should at least be able to respond in a timely manner to competition that arises. They must build a business model that can provide convenience and value—the two key parameters that drive customer need satiation. Brands which constantly adapt and evolve their business model will continue to grow.

If we look at the top 10 companies in terms of business growth, for the year 2019, we will find that most of them were start-ups founded some 20 years ago, which worked hard to create space and make a mark for themselves in the market by focussing on technology, innovation, and customer information. Of the top 5 companies, only Berkshire Hathaway Inc.—the company founded by Warren Buffett, which features at No. 5, is more than 50 years old. Similarly, in the list of top 10 companies, only 3 are over 50 years old, while 60 per cent of the companies featuring on the list are only about 20 years old. New businesses thrive on trying to find value by constantly researching and developing breakthrough technology that will help them carve out a niche of their own in the market. Many traditional businesses fail to spend adequate time and resources on doing research and developing technological innovations. Hence, they suddenly begin to lose market share, or their growth is impeded, as customer needs move to embrace more competitive options in the market space, where technological improvements and conveniences are offered.

Ford, which was once the market leader, is facing disruptive competition from Tesla, and has been replaced by Tesla as the market leader in the US. Likewise, the automotive sector in India and across the world is evolving with taxi aggregators bringing value to the customer by providing convenience and building cost efficiencies, resulting in a slowdown in the growth of the sector. In India, this is also a result of confusion created over the moving of technology, from April 2020, in diesels cars to Bharat Stage 6 emission technology, which would substantially raise the prices of diesel cars.

When a brand fails to evolve its business model in accordance with changing times in sync with technological development and innovative solutions in the market space that catch the customer eye and pocket, it will not be able to sustain its market share. A classic case in point is Kodak. Kodak became a leader as it innovated the market of personal photography by providing customers with personalized photographs that allowed them to capture and preserve personal moments for posterity, a privilege which, before Kodak's entry on the scene, was only available to professional photographers. Kodak expanded across the globe and set up its own retail stores which processed films and empowered the customer to have memories stored in hardcopy photographs.

The late 1990s saw the digital camera enter the market. However, with limited access to the Internet as well as a paucity of options to share pictures (as product penetration of the computer was quite low and the cost of digital cameras was quite high), Kodak went on, in 1999, to achieve its highest business growth.

The company also came up with its own version of the digital camera. However, Kodak was unable to gauge the rapid changes looming on the horizon. The year 2005 proved to be the year of digital transformation, as the cost of digital photography led to a massive fall in the margin structures that Kodak films had hitherto enjoyed. The margins fell from 80 per cent to single digits, and if that wasn't enough, Apple launched the iPhone in 2007, a phone that came equipped with high-end digital cameras providing the convenience of capturing and storing precious moments anywhere, anytime. With the changing market scenario, brands such as Fuji Film diversified their business and changed their business model and were able to sustain market share, whereas Kodak stuck to the retail format of its business, believing it had a retail business model which had historically given it 80 per cent returns. It was this complacency and failure to reinvent that ultimately led to bankruptcy. It is imperative that brands understand ever-changing market trends and revamp their business models so as to be a part of the renewed customer value perception.

Looking at the Indian market as well as international markets, in the current scenario, there are some key drivers that a brand must keep in mind if it wants to sustain its business:

1. **Invest in constant market research to keep finding value for the customer:** Businesses must keep their ears and eyes open to tap customer needs. They need to keep working on understanding emerging trends that could impact buying patterns. These could be competitive products, lifestyle changes, technological changes impacting the customer, and so on. For example, if more and more people begin to consume entertainment on offer via Amazon Prime, this could result in exposure to and awareness of other products of Amazon, which could help build customer trust required to migrate

from retail purchases to online purchases. This could impact retail brands, which may evaluate possibilities of collaboration with online portals such as Amazon so as not to lose out on customer loyalty.

2. **Understand that your business model could be replicated and ideate on how you will sustain your business:** Most businesses will find that what they offer to the customer can be replicated by someone else. Hence, their services offered and customer support systems should be timely as well as valuable to the customer in order to effectively build customer engagement as well as to understand their own weak points so as to strategically address these and build customer loyalty for their brand. This way, even when new competition surfaces, customers would stick to the brand they have been using until then.

   For example, the Patanjali group of companies build their business on the science of Ayurveda, forging a connect with the consumer based on the brand image of Baba Ramdev as well as the home-grown Swadeshi factor. They were able to scale up their business exponentially. However, after massive growth, they have started experiencing challenges in expanding market share in most of their products, except their flagship product, the toothpaste, Dant Kanti. This is because, one, multinational brands have entered the Ayurvedic product space, coming up with counter products and building a trust-based equation with the consumer, which makes the consumer believe in their product worth and value proposition. This in turn has curtailed the growth of Patanjali, which aggressively went ahead, offering products to the consumer who was willing to try their products. Yet, they failed to build customer loyalty by engaging with the existing consumer alone and working towards building the perceived qualitative value of their products.

3. **Work towards building value solutions for your customers through your products:** Stay ahead of competition by trying to understand your customer and keep building your product or service around his needs so as to foster customer engagement. Innovate your product in keeping with changing customer needs. For instance, with an increasing number of young couples working fast-paced, demanding schedules, their lifestyles are changing and home cooking is affected, whereby many of them prefer ordering in food. The next decade would see a major shift from home cooking to ready meals and home delivery of ready food. There is already a shift to food aggregator brands, with Swiggy and Zomato becoming dominant players. Even brands such as Uber have decided to leverage their data to expand their business through Uber Eats. The impact of this will be felt on grocery and retail food businesses in the times to come as more and more young couples get into the habit of ordering food.

   However, if these retail businesses play a role in massive education about the need for healthy home-cooked food, working towards enhanced awareness levels among consumers, this could help them maintain their market presence. For example, there has been a huge shift among the urban population towards vegan and healthy eating, with even many fine-dining restaurants offering vegan meals on the menu.

4. **Relationship-building with the consumer:** Customer engagement and customer intelligence is of paramount importance in competitive market spaces, and brands which are able to use customer information to build a relationship with the customer and add value will be able to provide a competitive edge to the customer experience. Google as a company has been able to build relationships with the consumer by using the myriad information it has access to, including customer interests, buying patterns, future needs,

etc., and that has been the sole driver behind Google pitching products and services relevant to customer interest, thereby building a substantial revenue stream for itself, making it one of the top companies in the world.

5. **Cost-effective value proposition marketing:** When a brand starts building a business model of cost-effective value proposition and is able to market that to a larger mass of population, it is able to open doors to the purchasing power of a much higher base of existing population. This helps it make inroads in markets of non-consumers of that category of products, thereby creating a sustainable, growing business, which directly leads to expansion of the market size of that business category. For example, Jio's success in the telecom market was based on its ability to convert non-users of mobile telephony into users by tapping the low penetration cost. Thereby, it has been able to increase data usage by providing a disruptive Internet access model which has changed the face of easy customer access to the Internet. The impact of this strategy is immense on the economic, political, and social scenario of the country. Consider how the ability of political parties to build their social image by using social media has helped them extensively redefine the political situation of the country. Similarly, there has been far-reaching economic and social impact because of wide access to easy, low-cost data in India.

Businesses need to understand that consumer needs are not dying; they are only shifting because of better solutions and intense competitive options available to the consumer. Most individual consumers would probably be spending more today than they were spending earlier; however, a deficit in building relationships with them results in major shifts. Even in recessionary markets, there are brands, such as DMart, that have carved out a sustainable growing market for themselves by focussing on offering cost-effective value propositions which enable them to build an emotional economic connect with the consumer.

This book aims to help you understand better how to build a sustainable business for your brand by educating you about the key drivers behind consumer needs. It promises to strengthen your ability to build a profitable business while protecting your business margins, which forms the foundation of sustainability and growth.

An Entrepreneur – The Ultimate Multitasker

STARTERS

1

The Two Bs That Drive Entrepreneurs

The life of an entrepreneur is by no means a cakewalk. But the echelons of history are rife with examples of entrepreneurs who went all out to chase their dream and came out tops in their endeavours. And the two overarching traits that they all share in common are a burning desire and unwavering belief.

Dhirubhai Ambani's story is the quintessential rags-to-riches story of a boy from an impoverished family setting up one of the biggest business empires in the country. He dropped out of school after Class 10 to take up a job in Yemen. However, looking at the limited opportunity it offered him, he decided to come back to India to establish a company in partnership with a cousin with a modest capital of ₹15000. They started trading in spices and yarns. Some years down the line, Dhirubhai, who, contrary to his cousin's cautious temperament, was a risk taker, decided to break up the partnership and set up his own business.

He found the yarn market very lucrative and chose to concentrate his energies there. He soon set up a manufacturing unit in Nadora, near Ahmedabad. Driven by a trademark feisty, indomitable spirit, he shunted back and forth between Mumbai and Ahmedabad, determined to manufacture the finest nylon. But on completing a large chunk of production, the wholesale marketers refused to pick up his goods because of the pressure they faced from existing yarn merchants. Not one to be deterred, he went on to sell directly to the retailer, creating the brand 'Vimal' under the Reliance textile banner.

Soon, he was minting money. He developed his wealth model further by foraying into the stock markets to generate more. The stock markets until then had been driven by financial institutes.

Dhirubhai revolutionised the markets by creating a retail equity market in the country, where he got the common man to invest in his company and earn profits from the investment. He was a remarkable businessman, endowed with enviable acumen that aided him in building, from almost nothing, one of the biggest conglomerates India has seen. He faced every challenge that came his way with the same never-say-die spirit. A business enterprise can thrive and flourish only with this kind of spirit and zest, for the challenges in establishing an enterprise will be innumerable but it is possible to confront them head-on and emerge victorious when one is armed with an indomitable will and a futuristic outlook.

Zomato, the one-stop solution to restaurants, home delivery and night life, albeit operating on an online platform, is another such success story, conceived in 2008 by two IIT Delhi alumni, Deepinder Goyal and Pankaj Chaddah, who gave up rosy careers to follow their dream. The inception for the business came from a simple idea the duo had when they observed people queuing up and waiting outside restaurants. With hardly any capital to start their business, armed only with unnerving belief in their idea, they began the journey to create an online guide to food and night life. Their passion, focused effort and perseverance helped them create a brand which today operates in over 1000 cities across 22 countries, which is quite a feat for a start-up that began operations only 10 years ago. The otherwise slow food industry has seen incremental growth with the online food market gathering momentum, following the rise in online ordering of food. With an increasing number of young couples caught up in hectic work schedules, the traditional, hands-on kitchen slowly made space for food ordered in, a trend further fuelled by the convenience of placing orders and receiving neatly packed food parcels. This young team of two spotted a golden opportunity and worked out a fantastic business model that has made this unicorn an aggressive player in the business of online food service.

So what is it that pushes these entrepreneurs to face everyday challenges and yet keep ploughing on? Let us look at some of the key drivers for entrepreneurial success:

1. **A burning desire to succeed:** As Napolean Hill puts it in his book *Think and Grow Rich,* people who have a burning desire to succeed are not deterred by the day-to-day challenges and they go all out to achieve their goals. In the above example of Dhirubhai Ambani, we see two stark cases in point, when he fought back the situation if it was not working for him. First, when he had no money to scale up his business, he innovatively thought of getting people to invest in his company, thereby creating a retail equity market for the first time in India. Second, when the wholesale market refused to pick up his readymade stock, he went directly to the retailer. It was nothing but the burning desire to succeed that kept him constantly thinking of solutions to address the problems he faced.

   There is no doubt that an entrepreneur will face umpteen challenges, as no business venture is a smooth ride, but in this journey, he must remain driven enough to work around every hurdle that may cross his path. At every stumbling step, he needs to rework strategies to achieve business goals in accordance with changing market situations, and this is where a singular burning desire will keep him going.

2. **Discipline:** The most important ingredient of success is the ability to stay disciplined. Most successful people talk of beginning the day early so as to have another two hours added to the working day. The discipline required to meticulously perform set tasks every day ensures the completion of work and helps deliver what is required and what has been promised. Warren Buffett, the world-renowned financial wizard, is a man of extraordinary self-discipline. It is his ability to be absolutely focused that has made him what he is today. As Alice Schroeder, a Warren Buffett biographer

states, "He ruled out paying attention to almost anything but business—art, literature, science, travel, architecture—so that he could focus on his passion."

Similarly, Tim Cook, the CEO of one of the world's most valued companies, Apple, is a man of extreme discipline and will power. He begins his day early, at 4 a.m., spending the first hour reading customer feedback. He clearly understands the importance of the dictum 'Customer is King', which is the barometer that has made Apple the first choice for millions of customers world-wide. Cook follows this practice religiously, followed by an hour's workout to beat the stress and keep him mentally agile and focused, to be able to have a productive day ahead.

Speaking about him in her book titled Haunted Empire: *Apple after Steve Jobs,* author Yukari Iwatani Kane says, "Cook demonstrated the same level of austerity and discipline in his life as he did in his work. He ate protein bars throughout the day and had simple meals like chicken and rice for lunch. His stamina was inhuman. He could fly to Asia, spend three days there, fly back, land at 7 a.m. at the airport and be in the office by 8.30, interrogating someone about some numbers."

A modern-day epitome of fitness, Indian cricket captain Virat Kohli is an exemplary model of discipline. However, the Virat we see today was not the same fit and disciplined person back in 2012. He had a bad season at the IPL, where he was eating the wrong things, drinking, and not sleeping well. It was then that he realised that if he wanted to be a top player able to sustain all three aspects of the game—balling, batting and fielding—he would need to be incredibly fit. The first two months were an absolute ordeal, as he went off sweets, gluten, wheat, and changed his eating habits. He actually felt like eating the bed sheet he slept on. But as time passed, he felt the difference in his mental and physical fitness owing to the regimen he followed. His fielding improved and his top physical and mental form paved the way for him to shoulder bigger responsibilities on the field and become the captain of the team.

3. **Confidence and belief:** Confidence and belief in one's idea is the spark that ignites the fire in the belly of successful entrepreneurs and urges them to chase what excites them. Their strong belief in their idea keeps them glued to it with single-minded direction, and it is also the reason why they are able to come up with wide-ranging solutions to the many hurdles they face in their entrepreneurial journey, as their confidence is never shaken in what they have set out to do. They are unfazed by the thought of failure en route; rather, they view any possibility of failure as learning and scope for innovation in the process.

   Ganesh Ram, the founder of Vivekananda English Training Academy, popularly known as VETA English Speaking Classes, had absolutely no means to start a business after he graduated. He was placed as a management trainee in the *Indian Express,* but decided to forego that job and instead create his own business, which he believed was his calling. Borrowing ₹500 from his mother to pay the deposit for an old bungalow in Chennai, available on a rent of ₹175 per month, he made up his mind to start Mathematics tuition classes. He had no idea nor experience as to how he would get students to come learn Mathematics from him, except his conviction that the business would allow him to pay rent for the premises. But he was confident and went scouting for students. He found three youngsters who had failed in the term exam. He committed to them that if they joined his coaching class, he would ensure that they passed in Mathematics. They agreed to join him at a fee of ₹30. However, after teaching them for a few days, he realised that paying the rent would still be difficult and he wondered who would fund him. He admitted to the three students that he needed more students, so could they each bring one more? They happily brought two new students each, so that in the first month itself, Ganesh had nine students and earned ₹270, not only paying his rent but also earning a profit!

His journey was filled with challenges when scalability became a problem, when franchisees used his brand name and he could do nothing as he was not aware about having to register a brand name. He was not aware about taxation either. Yet, the journey of creating a 60-crore business helped him learn how to deal with each hurdle and come out a winner until he decided to sell off his business to the TIME group.

The other day, I was reading about a boy named Nitesh Yadav, who hailed from the small town of Alwar in Rajasthan, who went all out to create various apps and also an artificial intelligence platform called 'Exam Mitra' to study while using Facebook. He is all of 15 years of age and came in contact with a smartphone at the age of 13. Inspired by another creator of apps from his home town, Nitesh developed the confidence that he too could create one. He went ahead and used Google to learn about app-making, ultimately creating many useful apps. Coming from a family where owning a smartphone was not an easy thing, his confidence and belief in himself kept him going.

4. **Open-mindedness:** Entrepreneurship is a journey packed with new learnings every day and entrepreneurs need to be open-minded enough to see the opportunities, advice and ideation coming in from people around them. Howard Schultz, on a trip to Milan as a young marketer working for a Seattle coffee bean roaster, got an idea for upscale espresso cafes, such as the ones he saw in Italy. His employer showed no interest in coffee shops but agreed to fund him. He also gave Howard their brand name, Starbucks. Thus was born the super successful

coffee chain we see expanding everywhere today. And it began simply as a new idea that came to the young man who kept an open mind.

The story of Marico, India's own answer to MNCs across the world, is based on having an open mind while evaluating business. They have created their own success story by offering products that are niche and ethnic in nature, where large MNCs are not really active. Marico saw success in establishing a branded oil market in the hair care segment which is largely a South Asian need and did not feature on the radar of MNC focus. The brand's foray in South Africa, too, is focused on the ethnic hair category which is growing at a scorching pace.

Harsh Mariwala, Executive Director and Founder, Marico, once said, "I can't fight with MNCs in their primary categories. So what is a fringe category for them is the main category for us. I want to be the market leader in whatever category I am in. The trick is to identify areas where MNCs won't enter."

They entered the baby care market, but realising the huge competition therein and the transitory nature of product usage, they exited the market and decided to focus on products which would help them be market leaders. Theirs is a ₹5000-crore brand, no mean feat for a brand which started operations as recently as 1988.

5. **Competitiveness:** Entrepreneurship requires spirited belief that one can do things and that one is probably better off than many others to work on the idea at hand. Once that happens, people start seeing an opportunity. This quality keeps entrepreneurs going. The story of how Thyrocare was born reflects the importance of this competitive spirit. Dr A Velumani, the founder of Thyrocare, worked for 15 years at Bhabha Atomic Research Centre (BARC). He saw many people whom he had trained to take lab samples go on to flourish in

life. At one point, he realised that he could do well too, but only if he quit his job and started his own business, and so, without consulting his wife, he left his job. His entire family was disturbed by this sudden act, but his wife believed in him and became a solid pillar of support for him. He managed to create a ₹3300-crore business empire out of the ₹2 lakh he had originally invested in the business. Had he not taken the drastic step of quitting his job, believing in his own competitive strength, he would never have realised his full potential. But innate potential gets realised only when there is business acumen that supports the idea, helping entrepreneurs work relentlessly to create what they know they can do.

6. **Persistence:** Persistence is the most crucial element in success; it is only through undying passion, determination and persistence to keep going that entrepreneurs are able to script success stories.

   Digressing a little, I want to make mention of an interesting story I have read and heard so many times. It is the story of a baby elephant whose leg is chained to a wooden post. He tries and tries to tug and pull away from it, but when he does not manage to move much, he sits down. As time goes by, he keeps growing and his strength increases too, but his mind is conditioned to believe that once he has been tied to the post, he can't break free, and so he stays put there. We all know that the elephant is a powerful animal with massive strength, enough to uproot full-grown trees and upturn vehicles. But with a mind so conditioned, that refuses to stay open, as seen in this story, even an elephant is not able to evaluate its own strength.

   I have a three-year-old pug at home, and it is pure delight to see his persistence. We often tie his leash to a handle, but he has learnt the art of doggedly pulling and tugging at his end of the leash to free himself. There are times when we tie him to the heavy sofa bottom, or a wrought iron stand, and yet, by continuously exerting his strength, he manages to unleash himself. I once decided to get innovative and looped one end of the leash through the round hole in the drawer handle in such a manner that he would need to cut the leash to release himself. But let me tell you, the little fella just didn't give up even then! He managed to break that shoe cupboard handle made of three steel pieces by repeatedly gnawing at the handle and tugging furiously at it. His spirit is an inspiration to all of us at home, as he never gives up, and it is this spirit that has allowed him to win over any situation he finds himself in. Whatever the challenge we may present to him, he manages to find his way out of it so that, often enough, in the middle of the night, we turn in our bed to find a cuddly ball of fur snuggling up to us.

Everyone knows Hershey's chocolates today, but when Milton Hershey first set out in his candy production career, he was a nobody. After being fired from an apprenticeship with a printer, Hershey started three different candy-related ventures, and he saw all of them fail.

As a final attempt, Hershey founded the Lancaster Caramel Company, after which he began seeing enormous results. Believing in his vision to produce milk chocolate for the masses, he eventually founded the Hershey Company and became one of the most well-known names in the industry.

7. **People skills:** An entrepreneur has to be a people's person; he can't do it all alone. He needs a team to work with, and he also needs to collaborate with vendors from other businesses to create partnerships for growth and development. K V Kamath, the stellar CEO of ICICI, is credited with having created a whole lot of leaders in the Indian finance industry.

   He had a knack for identifying talent and he mentored his recruits by giving them challenging assignments and empowering them to take decisions. It was this ability that helped him pick out many young protégés in their 30s, and he groomed them to become leaders who would drive India's financial growth. Chanda Kochhar went on to become ICICI's CEO, Shikha Sharma came to lead Axis Bank as CEO, Kalpana Morparia joined J.P. Morgan as CEO, V Vaidyanathan became CEO of Future Capital Holdings, to name a few. It was this pool of talent under Kamath's able leadership which was able to catapult ICICI to the pinnacle of success and make it the largest bank in India. But Kamath was not someone who mentored people by building a personal rapport with his proteges by socialising with them; he believed in establishing a one-on-one rapport of trust and respect with them, having brief meetings where he set expectations and then laid the playing field open to them to take the journey forward. His style of empowerment is what helped these talented people stretch themselves to their limits to deliver.

The story of Wells Fargo is another shining example of how the right people can make a difference. As Jim Collin describes in his book *Good to Great,* Wells Fargo began a 15 year spectacular performance stint in 1983. The foundation for this was laid in the early 1970s, when the then CEO, Dick Cooley, began building one of the best management teams according to Warren Buffett. Cooley foresaw that the banking industry would eventually undergo huge changes, so instead of mapping strategies for change, he and the chairman, Ernie Arbuckle, began building the right team by injecting an endless stream of talent into the company. They hired outstanding people whenever and wherever they found them, even without any specific role in mind.

Cooley stated that this was the way to forge the future as, if he was not smart enough to see the future, they would, and they would also be flexible enough to deal with the changes that came along the way. He was proved right. When banking deregulation occurred, no bank handled the changes better than Wells Fargo. At a time when banking sector stocks fell 59 per cent behind the general stock market, Wells Fargo outperformed the market by over three times. Carl Reichardt Jr, who became the CEO, attributed the bank's success to the people around him, people he had inherited from Cooley.

Later, nearly every member of the Cooley-Reichardt era executive team went on to become the CEO of a major company. Wells Fargo's approach was simple—get the best people, build them to become the best managers in the industry, and then accept the fact that some of them would be recruited as CEOs of other companies.

8. **Learning ability:** In technology and business, it is imperative that an entrepreneur continues to hone his skills to understand the changing dynamics of the market. If he is willing to constantly learn and explore, he can de-risk his business and create newer opportunities for himself.

   India's most famous actor, one who has earned the sobriquet of 'Legend', Amitabh Bachchan is a classic example of how persistent efforts combined with the right attitude to reinvent and adapt with the times can change one's destiny. When he began his career, he had a series of flops. He was never a conventional chocolate boy hero, but he didn't think that was a deterrent in his chosen path and he redefined the mainstream actor's place in Indian cinema as the angry young man, creating a larger-than-life image for himself. When he entered the political scene, he was tainted by the Bofors scandal. He was unable to play the lead with the same finesse as he aged. Furthermore, in 1992, he decided to sponsor the Miss World pageant in Bangalore and his company ABCL was hit with huge financial losses. People started writing him off. Here was a man who could have declared himself bankrupt, but he did not do that. Instead, he went to the banks who had financed him and said, "Give me time, I will pay back every penny I owe you." He reinvented himself, changing his looks and image, and did what no actor in mainstream cinema would do then—he decided to be part of a TV show.

India witnessed a revolution in viewership as *Kaun Banega Crorepati* debuted on TV. The streets would be empty at night as people would stay glued to their sets, watching the charming Amitabh Bachchan make the dreams of many ordinary people come true through the power of the prize money on offer.

At 77 today, he remains a legend as he keeps updating himself, effectively using social media to be on top in his chosen field, with people still writing scripts for him. Many of his counterparts faded away into oblivion in spite of being very talented, as they did not constantly work to innovate themselves and they did not stretch themselves to learn new ways and means to keep things going for them. Amitabh Bachchan's story is a veritable testimony to the fact that we are ourselves the creators of our destiny, through our thoughts and efforts to achieve the goals we set for ourselves.

Entrepreneurs who are good human beings are able to create long-term success, as they are able to attract good manpower and partners who support and help them during stressful situations. Successful entrepreneurship is all about being clear about your purpose, staying focused and disciplined, having the ability to evaluate things with an open mind, and gauging what will work best for you. Perhaps the most critical requirement is the ability to synergise with people to create platforms and associations to partner success.

2

The Business Plan

Most businesses are born in the vision of an idea which will be able to garner consumer interest. What kind of business idea is the right one for you? How do you tap the real potential in an idea, and avoid putting your energies behind one that may not prove sustainable and profitable? The answer is different for every individual, as you need to love the field you are venturing into and you must know it well. For a business to be suitable, it must be something you like to do and can do well. You should have the ability to leverage your core strengths and assess how they will fit in best with the opportunities available to begin your entrepreneurial journey. There may be a wide range of skills and knowledge that you would need to obtain or sharpen to be able to sustain the business model you adopt.

There should be a reasonably large number of people interested on a steady basis in the business idea or product you choose. It should be able to command a price in the market that will cover all your expenses and overheads as well as offer a healthy, profitable return on investments made. You should have the money to keep the business afloat, or the ability to raise money to keep it running until it starts delivering profits. You need to earmark a plan for business goals to be achieved, keeping in mind all the above aspects, especially the ability to sustain the business. The plan must encapsulate what has to be achieved, the timeline for the same, and the ways and means to achieve the set goals within the allotted time frames.

The only way to create a fool-proof, successful business model is to constantly benchmark objectives to be achieved and track the progress being made. If there is any variance in what has been set as part of the plan and what is actually achieved, then it is important to know beforehand what actions need to be taken to correct such variance, or have an alternative strategy ready to keep things on track.

The first step in executing any business idea is definitely identifying what is the right business proposition. What is the product/service you will offer, who will be your target audience, how will you identify the target audience, will you look at need creation or will you concentrate largely on a market segment that is already aware of its needs, what innovation would the customer experience with you, and why would he buy from you—these are some of the questions you need to have answers for, to start with. How will you market your offering and drive people towards your business? What are the key business investments you would need to make, where are the funds you would need to make these investments and what is the working capital required? What is the manpower support you would require, who would be in your core team to help you drive your plan forward and how would you hold this team together in fulfilling your vision? These are the next array of questions to ask yourself. Then comes the most important question—what are the margins in the business, what is the break-even risk time, do you have the finances and the will to hold on to that, as also the ability to adapt and innovate in a dynamically changing market scenario?

Notwithstanding these key questions you need to evaluate, there has to be a Unique Selling Proposition (USP) that will work as a differentiator and help you build your product in the market. Take the example of Jio, a Mukesh Ambani group venture. It was a late entrant in the telecom sector which was bleeding with low margins with hardly four players of some dominance left in the market, even though mobile telephony with data plans are an absolute necessity for mass consumption. In such a scenario, it would have been impossible for Jio to make a foray in the market, but they came up with IP-based technology, believing strongly that the future of telecom was data, realising the potential of data which wasn't unlocked by the prevalent crop of telecom operators who were focusing more on voice than on data services. This was a paradigm shift, but it enabled Jio to take on the market with a proposition that was hitherto largely untapped. Jio also realised that investment in the infrastructure was assured if they offered free services for the first three months of usage, followed by another three-month period, as they would acquire customers who would end up paying ₹2000 for the handset in many cases to avail of three months of free service along with free Internet access—an offer which was unprecedented in Indian mobile telephony. Jio created a revolution and disrupted the market to pull customers towards it. People opted for it based on the promise of three months of free service, and with extension of duration of free service, there was further rise in the number of users. But the brand had already got the initial amount of handset money/deposit which helped to build a sizeable cash flow as well as user base. However, this was only possible because of the product strength of providing high-speed Internet access, allowing consumers to greatly benefit from it. Moreover, the high-speed Wi-Fi Internet access sales model was built on the same revenue principle. This gave them a cash flow of ₹4500 per customer, as well as a subscriber base of regular clients after three months who would continue using their network. In fact, practically every third person has a Jio SIM card today.

Compare this with Tata Docomo's entry into the telecom market which adopted a path of slashing prices, making all operators follow in their footsteps and slash their prices as well because they wanted to stay competitive. As a result, profit margins came down drastically and all operators started looking at value-added services to enhance their margins. Docomo was not a winner either in such a market condition as the price slashing didn't really benefit them. They did manage to acquire customers in the short run, but it wasn't good enough for the company to sustain their business model for a long time, as it was no different in USP from other operators and it played the low-price-per-call card, which was immediately adopted by the other, existing telecom operators. The folly lay in the huge capital expenditure investment that is required in telecom and wafer-thin margins which prolonged break-even point for the business, whereby adequate cash flow planning and operating profitability had to be clearly planned. I have seen how a tight cash flow management with protection of bottom lines in a business is a clear essential for any business to survive in the face of ever-changing market dynamics. It is difficult to keep infusing fresh money every year if the margins are not protected, and the probability of business delivery based on the plan is not always achieved as, at times, market forces are not in our control. A volatile economy needs to be factored in when taking risks in any business, but these have to be calculated risks, keeping in mind Plan B and Plan C.

A business idea, before it is implemented, should be evaluated in depth. There has to be enough homework done in terms of the product/service being offered. Some of the key things to be kept in mind are understanding, to begin with, why people would be interested in one's idea, why they would put money into it. To get them to take interest in the idea, there has to be a clear business plan in place.

I have found that the 7 Cs (illustration follows) need to be the drivers behind a comprehensive business plan.

The other day, I read somewhere that more than 80 per cent of businesses that start are shut down, and one of the main reasons is the lack of a comprehensive plan which needs to be executed. From experience, I have learnt that to achieve anything, there has to be a defined way of doing it, factoring in the market forces. The law of probability pegs success higher if the plan has been worked out comprehensively. The best of products have become a success only when the right business margins are applied, when there is a good marketing strategy in place, the right people to drive it, and so on. Some excellent products were unable to create a market for themselves as the team didn't work to create a sound business plan to help the product achieve its full potential.

I believe the 7 Cs are a great foundation stone to help work on all aspects of the product growth cycle in a business. They are outlined below:

1. **Consumer connect:** Who will be my target audience and why will he buy my product—this constitutes the first of the Cs. If I am entering an established business segment, what are the differentiators in my product and how will the consumer connect to the brand I offer with the help of these differentiators. For example, let us take the case of the Patanjali group. Their products are so similar in packaging and styling to existing market products, but the uniqueness of their brand was built on the brand image of Baba Ramdev. He had a mass following, especially with the middle class and the rural market, and his strong market appeal helped to build an audience which was willing to try their products. His brand appeal was made effective further by playing the Indian card of patriotism, which allowed the audience to develop an emotional link with the brand. Along with this, they played the pricing card well, stating that they were passing on the best prices in the market to the consumer. Patanjali's advertising hit out directly at multinationals and established foreign brands, resulting in a swadeshi connect with its target group, making it one of the fastest growing companies in recent times.

   In spite of being a late entrant in most product markets, Baba Ramdev's products established themselves on the strength of 'Dantkanti', an Ayurvedic toothpaste that found many takers, and the brand scaled up the business, creating a connect with the customer ethos of patriotism and affordable pricing.

   There are so many other products that were unable to connect to the consumer in spite of being good products. In 2011, Hewlett Packard introduced the HP TouchPad and its mobile operating system webOS, but it was unable to make any significant value proposition to the consumer. It was supposed to be akin to the iPad, but it's rough edges could have been modelled better. Since it was unable to build any connect with the consumer and create a differentiation for itself, in spite of being a decent product, it was removed from the market within two months of its launch because of poor sales.

So you see, it is imperative to have a clearly thought out connect with the consumer and make that the foundation of your brand, because people buy only when they emotionally connect with a product or service.

2. **Claim:** What we claim is the core of our product will help us determine how we position it. Research and market analysis is vital before we draft a business plan for what we are offering, to assess whether the marketing, positioning and pitch are appropriate to attract the target audience, and to fine-tune the proposition as required, in such a manner that it will make the customer buy. A sampling with the target audience will help us identify and understand the gaps in our pitch, proposition and product.

   Once we are clear on the product pitch and positioning, we need to work on product development. For any concept or physical product, there has to be a detailed study on how to go about developing it. The best part about the times we live in is that almost every kind of information is available online.

   If you need to come up with ideas on how to take your product forward, figure out what people in that space are doing. What is the pricing, what is the marketing pitch they are making, what are the channels they are using to get hold of the customer—these are essentials to keep in mind when planning product margins. Furthermore, studying these factors will give a clear understanding of your product in the market space and will aid in conceptualising your idea or product, in evaluating what is special about it that will make the consumer buy it. The 'why' must be impactful with defined reasons—why people will invest in the product or service and what are the tangible benefits available to them if they do. Let's look at examples of products which created a pathway for themselves by working on the needs of the consumer.

The insurance sector, which grew post-liberalisation in the late 1990s in India, had marketing appeal in two clear propositions. The first and foremost was fear—if something happened to an individual, what would be the security provided to the family. The second factor that played a role was that people in India were looking to save tax found solace under the Income Tax 80G saving scheme, and so in this respect, there was scope to expand in the market. There were two to three major, traditional investment tools available to the masses, namely, the Public Provident Fund (PPF), the National Saving Scheme and Post Office schemes. The insurance sector saw an opportunity here and used their claim of providing security to one's family in eventuality of anything untoward happening to the policy holder, and he could also save tax under the 80G benefit. The late 90s saw the insurance sector grow exponentially as private players began to grow the market. Life Insurance Corporation of India (LIC) also redefined its pitch to introduce new products, keeping these two propositions in mind, with fear becoming the bigger proposition, thereby maintaining its market share.

If you are able to develop your product keeping the below pointers in mind, you have a perfect recipe for making your product or service successful.

- **Differentiation and USPs:** A product or service must have uniqueness which differentiates or distinguishes it from other options available.
- **Appeals to the masses:** Your product or service will have a higher chance at success if it can be customised to suit

a larger mass of people. If it has a market for students, housewives as well as businessmen, chances of success are great. If you are starting a new business, it is better to have a large mass product appeal. An established business can experiment by coming out with niche products, addressing a select audience.

- **Useful proposition:** Your product or service must address a need where it can be useful or will help solve a problem. For example, the success of coaching classes in India was based on the need of students to qualify for various entrance exams in a highly competitive market. Coaching classes went to great lengths to get a few good students who could become their marketing tool in order to attract the larger mass of students to aspire and achieve what past students had done.

- **Pricing:** Is the pricing appealing enough to fit the requirements of people? If not, the product must have high value perception which is exclusive to it to be able to create a niche market for itself.

- **Great results:** If the results or benefits of usage can be demonstrated in the marketing stage, chances of the product doing well are better. When I worked for the Swedish cosmetic company Oriflame and we gave a product demonstration to customers, say for a face wash, they ended up buying that product as well as other products in that range which enhanced its results, in spite of the pricing being more than the average product price of competitive products, because they saw first-hand tangible results which helped to build value.

- **Simple to use:** The product or service must be such that it can be used by most people. Complex products may attract fewer customers.

Hence, it is important to make the claims unique and beneficial and to work on product development to create a genuinely good and useful product for all users.

3. **Communication:** The third most important aspect is about communicating to the consumer who will connect with you once he gets to know about your claims. It is worthwhile to think about how you will communicate with this audience. Most brands have been built by resorting to aggressive advertising and visibility. "Joh dikhta hai woh bikta hai" (what is seen gets sold) is the marketing mantra that many brands swear by and it is the key to their success. But it is imperative that the communication must carry the message that will connect to the consumer and will prod him to buy what you have to offer. Overplaying a particular message in the same format will lead to it being treated like a blind spot. There are many instances where a brand comes up with a huge marketing plan without studying who is the target audience and how the brand will build an emotional connect with the consumer and urge him to buy the product. Most successful marketing campaigns have been built around effective communication. The Pidilite story of success had its seeds in the rustic yet innovative Fevicol advertisement campaigns which targeted the carpenter, the contractor and the consumer who would pay for the product. They got the campaign right by reaching the right target group at all levels, and by conducting promotional activities and giving training to the carpenters, they built a beautiful business model.

   They pioneered furniture design books which carpenters and contractors started carrying with them, as at that time there was no Internet nor were furniture design books easily accessible. The product had a monopoly in the market and its strong advertising campaign helped what was practically a one-product (Fevicol) company to build a business empire in the adhesive market as the advertisements bearing the slogan 'Fevicol ka mazboot jod hai, tootega nahi' had a wonderful recall value. These campaigns made the brand even stronger as they came up with products like M-Seal, Fevistick, Dr Fixit, etc.

However, in today's times, it is not enough to merely communicate. In a world that is thriving on the digital platform, where multiple platforms are available to connect with audiences and communicate with them—something that was not so easy to do in earlier times—if you are able to engage with people by touching an emotional chord or a humorous chord, you will get many people to share your communication onward so that its reach widens. The Filter Copy campaign on YouTube created by Pocket Aces is an innovative marketing strategy of mixed media for all things shareable, including interesting articles, relatable videos, funny memes, where the integration of brands is done seamlessly with stories built around people. Their video content and storyline centres on couples, friends, families and their lives, adding masala to the copywriting by adding interesting characters and a relatable human angle to the storylines.

Content communication must have relevant communication for different consumers based on their level in the product sales cycle. There are three types of consumers, whom I call the ABC (Awarness Level Customers, Buyer Level Customers, Consideration Level Customers) type of customers. Brand connect and communication must address the product pitch based on their stage in the sales cycle.

Awareness Level Customers — Buyer Level Customers — Consideration Level Customers

The ABC Customers

- **Awareness level:** There will be some consumers who are not aware of the product. They may have a dormant need, and to address this consumer, the communication must be directed towards creating a desire to buy the product by educating them on the benefits the consumer will get.

- **Buyer level:** This kind of customer is a hot lead. He is already scouting in the market to buy, and he needs immediate communication, otherwise you may miss him. The content communication must clearly bring out the benefits and differentiations/testimonial of happy consumers and it must be offer-based communication.

- **Consideration level:** The third kind of consumer is one who is considering buying a product. He may not have decided on what he will buy, but is evaluating available options. Here, it is important that the USPs that differentiate the product from other options available in the market should be the core message of the communication.

  If a brand creates content differently for different kinds of consumers based on their stage of buying, the possibility of making the right connect with a larger mass of consumers is possible, as it will then be relevant content for each section of the audience.

4. **Competition:** You need to understand the competition in the space of your business and gauge what will be the differentiating factors that will help build a market for your products in that space. If you are a late entrant in the segment, you can still create a market for yourself as Jio did, by bringing the kind of value to the consumer which the competition was not providing.

   Similarly, the bottled water market was built on the consumer's need to have clean drinking water. When new players wanted to build market share, brands such as Coca-Cola South

Pacific launched a new Glaceau-branded water—low calorie, flavoured, sparkling spring water—customised for health-conscious female consumers in the age bracket of 30 and above. Another similar product in this range came from Refresh, an Australian company which produced a 'super-oxygenated' water, called Oxyfresh, containing Himalayan crystal salt and 700 per cent more oxygen than normal water. These products were targeted at customers aiming to have a healthy lifestyle. Increasing consumer awareness and brand consciousness led to an increase in the demand for branded bottled water. Premium bottled waters differentiated themselves from the average bottled water in the market based on factors such as precisely calibrated pH levels, mineral content, purity and presentation. The brand image was created in such a way that it was projected as a luxury good, encouraging consumers to spend more than what is required on a bottle of water. Globally, premium brands such as Nestlé, Danone, and Gerolsteiner now account for 40 per cent of all premium water sales, and they are also slowly making their way to even price-sensitive markets such as India.

The growing number of health-conscious consumers across the world is a key factor driving the demand for bottled water. Greater levels of health awareness among consumers has made bottled water manufacturers focus on products that contain minerals and vitamins along with new flavours. Bisleri, the Indian pioneer of bottled water, has focused on building its brand value and differentiation through expansion of its business, by coming out with Vedica, a natural spring water brand which it claims comes with the richness of underground water minerals acting as a natural antacid.

Given rising living standards, many people are switching from aerated drinks to functional and flavoured water that is calorie-free, caffeine-free, or free from other artificial ingredients.

This factor has resulted in many new players entering the market and trying to cash in on this particular consumer need creation.

Imagine you have a new product and you want to target a consumer from a different service, to make him move to your category which may be technologically and value-wise absolutely different. For example, you may be offering a service that has to get the consumer to move up by notches in terms of expenses or value creation. Take, for instance, the laser hair reduction market which was targeting a consumer using the method of waxing to remove body hair. The product, price, proposition, and end result—all are of a different category. But a market for the product can still be created by building the right benefit analysis based on convenience and long-term value proposition.

Some of the things one needs to bear in mind while launching a new product in a highly competitive market are:

- **Room for your product:** In an overcrowded market which has a plethora of products, you must look through available market research findings to see if there is room for your product, otherwise you will be eating into market shares of existing players and pushing down the margins for yourself and others. Understand the scope of expansion of the target audience to understand expansion of the market size.

- **Create USPs for your product:** Create differentiations for your products, so that the consumer knows why he must buy your product. Test your product well. Frito Lays launched a product called Wow, which spoke about fat-free wafers, but the product was detrimental to the customer as it could not be digested easily and resulted in diarrhoea for the consumer and had to be withdrawn from the market. Development and launch of products must be done after adequate testing, lest such launches prove detrimental to a business. So a brand must work on carrying out sufficient research while coming up with their USPs.

- **Communicate with your target audience effectively:** Know who your target audience is and how you can strike an emotional chord with them, how you can draw their attention to your product. Pick up carefully those channels of advertising which will help you reach your target group and work on creating effective content to reach that audience. If you have a product for youth today, maybe Instagram may work better compared with some other media platforms, whereas a product targeting middle-class housewives may work more effectively on the Facebook advertising platform. Understand your target group and your product and accordingly create relevance there.

5. **Cost:** Cost is the most important variant in the product life cycle, as pricing and margins are calculated based on direct and indirect costs along with operating overheads. What this means is that when a product price is to be finalised, the parameters to be borne in mind are competitive pricing as well as manufacturing/trading costs along with taxes, operating overheads, such as rent, salary, administrative costs, etc. It must also factor in projected volumes along with the contingency plans on how to go forward in case these projected volumes are not met.

   At times, you may face a situation wherein, considering the direct and indirect costs incurred, your pricing will need to be higher than the market price in order for you to make sizeable margins so as to have a profitable business. In that case, you must decide what value you will build into the product to allow it to create a space for itself in the market. You may want to have an initial, in-built sales promotion cost as part of the introductory offer, to make the customer try your product.

It would help you sustain the business in the long run if your product is built on clear, competitive, differentiated pitching, which will make the consumer try you out. It is much better to price your product at a cost that covers your viability, but at the same time to build a certain value which the brands you are competing with are not offering. Then when you bring out an introductory offer, at least some people will give it a shot. Tangible benefits and value added to your product or service based on in-depth research will help you initiate the process whereby people see value in your product, and that in turn will create the initiation of a brand which you will then have to nurture through effective communication and value enhancement. As stated above, the two approaches to pricing are cost-plus pricing and value-based pricing.

Before finalising which is the best approach to adopt, one would need to:

- Understand market price sensitivity, to gauge whether there is scope for building cost-plus pricing with the right margins, or whether the market is open to value building. If not, the costs will have to be controlled in the first place so that you have a viable product.
- Furthermore, in a product life cycle, prices can seldom be fixed for long; they need to change with the dynamic market and in keeping with the competition's pricing strategy.

6. **Cash flow:** Closely linked with the aspect of cost is the element of cash flow planning in your business. You need to look carefully at the amount of money you would need to drive your business to the market. There has to be enough working capital set aside for sustaining a business in adverse circumstances. The business plan must encapsulate all costs, ranging from rent, manpower and administrative costs, marketing and financial outlay, taxes, etc., and also look at

expected monthly returns to tide over these expenses. The break-even period must be calculated and accordingly, cash flow must be planned. A close watch needs to be maintained on the defined sales price and the quantified numbers to be achieved in order to keep the business plan on track. It is important to build the right margins for business to flourish. There has to be a decent margin maintained in business operations to ensure profits. A leading global business centre, when they launched their service in India, took on a real estate specialist as their commercial head, who wove the very fabric of the organisation keeping the real estate costs low. The business enjoyed profit margins of 80 per cent plus, because the core cost in the business model was the rent, and saving on that made the Indian arm of operations the most profitable venture globally.

Compare this with another player that started operations in the same business. They opened centres paying extremely high rentals as the people who negotiated were not Indian locals and they didn't foresee that the backbone of the business (the cost of rent) they were dealing with was per European standards. So, in spite of having an excellent team which gave them almost 100 per cent occupancy in the real estate crisis period of 2008-09, they were unable to sustain the business for long as the profitable workstation cost that they had built of ₹ 60000 to ₹100000, thanks to shifting market dynamics, came down to ₹25000 to ₹40000, which proved unsustainable as the margins in the business were low. They were forced to sell off their business. Meantime, the other player, in spite of running occupancy rates of 50 per cent, was able to sustain the business thanks to lower costs incurred in the same business model.

Hence, a business plan must have a contingency plan for a change in market situation, in lieu of considerations such as government regulations, financial crisis in the market, etc.

However, one needs to know that even profitable companies can run out of cash if they spend too much on inventory, debt repayment, new equipment and assets, as these are not a part of the profit-and-loss statement. A company must plan business expansion keeping in mind the cash flow situation.

Furthermore, inventory management must be based on the EOQ method, i.e., the Economic Order Quantity, which is the order quantity that minimises total holding and ordering costs for the year.

The revenue forecast must be done taking into account the worst-case scenario while planning the cash flow, because variances therein could lead to a serious cash flow crisis. There must be an emergency fund that equals at least six months of the working capital needs in a running business. A new business must formulate its business plan based on revenue planning, and revenue achievement must be constantly monitored to lead the business to a position of stability and viability.

It is imperative that one builds a business keeping the costs low and makes decent margins. If the margins against competitive prices are low, one must build the product with appropriate value additions and differentiators whereby the consumer perceives a real value benefit.

7. **Core team:** A business needs people to drive it. One cannot drive the business alone; one would still need a team that must align itself with the vision and plan laid out and work together on the same. A successful business needs a dynamic team which will brainstorm, execute and deliver the business goals. The most important reason why diversity is required in a team is that people with different work experiences and exposure to different aspects of the business are able to add value in diverse ways towards building the business. During the 1980s

and 90s, the *Hindustan Times*, which was the leader in the print business in Delhi, slowly began to lose its leadership status in Delhi, as the team who had been in media for years had grown complacent and over-confident about their leadership status. *The Times of India*, a western newspaper, was over the years spreading its wings across the country, and by the late 1980s, it was aggressively capturing the market. The *Hindustan Times* began to lose it market share. It was then that they appointed Rajeev Verma in 2004, who came with rich cross-sectoral experience in varied brands, including Unilever, Nestlé, and Whirlpool. He began reconstructing the company by building a team which could boast of diverse experience across industries, so as to infuse new ideas, remove the spirit of complacency and work on new ways to increase revenue and turnover with a spirit of 'We can do it'. HT Media's management team began to become a rich mix of veterans from media and top leaders from non-media sectors, from both India and abroad. This reflected the company's desire to be the best by leveraging diverse strengths.

HT grew by leaps and bounds in various businesses, growing the vernacular segment with *Hindustan*, and creating big national brands, including *Mint*, Fever 104, Radio Nasha, Shine.com. The new team under Mr Verma's guidance was responsible for the focus on new business, such as events and key marketing solutions, advertising for equity, and education, as well as major international collaborations with partners such as Virgin Radio, Burda, *The Wall Street Journal* and *The Washington Post*. The company transformed from a babu company to a corporate. There was immense corporatisation of the company under the new leader's aegis. He changed the culture of the organisation definitively by bringing in the right team. The company went on to achieve more than five times its original business turnover, making it to the big league and becoming one of the finest media companies in the industry.

What we learn from this is that although most businesses take birth via a business idea, through innovative thinking and looking at an idea or product that already exists in the market, it is absolutely essential to have a scientific process in place to evaluate and crystallise the business idea before going into operations full steam. It is a detailed business plan that helps an organisation chart out strategy optimally, and when a business plan works on the 7 Cs, it will be able to build the primary framework that is required for the enterprise to embark on its journey.

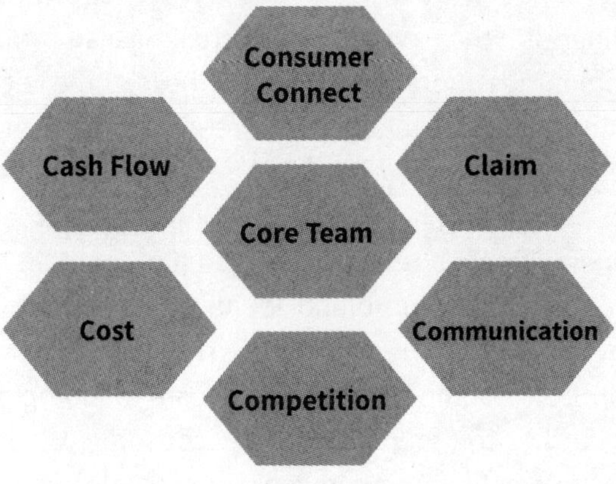

The 7Cs

3

Brand Development

The very reason why a brand comes into existence is to make people aware of a particular product. To make a consumer capable of identifying and recognising the product based on the brand name and thereby have a relationship going with the consumer, such that the consumer becomes a loyal user of the product—this is exactly what branding aims to do.

Branding is the process of creating an image/logo/ name (sometimes more than one of these three elements in combination) that registers in the mind of the consumer so that he differentiates what they mean to him and whether they fit into the space of satiating his needs. Branding strives to attract the consumer and create a relationship with him to retain his loyalty as a buyer and user. The brand identity is shaped by creating consistent marketing strategies based on the positioning the brand wants to assume to establish its core branding principles. These are further communicated to the consumer via advertising campaigns to create a brand image. For example, when it comes to the Tata group of companies, the first thought that comes to our mind in terms of what the brand stands for is trust. To create this association, the brand should have lived this vision across all its engagement platforms with the consumer. Branding is developed at every aspect of customer engagement, which may include interaction with sales personnel, customer service teams, what people see and hear about the organisational culture, the management teams, the advertising campaign(s), customer feedback and reviews, what they see and hear via social media, and so on.

Moreover, a brand needs to be sensitive to what social, economic, and cultural issues it stands for. Uber (the cab service) faced a brand crisis when, one after another, it treaded on controversial grounds as it took stands on the Muslim immigration ban in the US. There were cases of sexual abuse slapped on the top management, which was aggravated with a video that went viral of the CEO berating an Uber driver. Both the president and the CEO had to step down and a new chief branding officer was appointed to stabilise the situation and get the brand to build back its credibility.

Good branding is all about 'pull'. A brand that is able to connect with the consumer by understanding his needs will be able to pull consumers towards it. It is not merely an exercise in shaping the strategy and positioning adopted for the product or service; it is about what the brand stands for, what it resonates with at every level of consumer connect. If it lives up to the image of its core brand identity at every level, the brand will develop a strong connect with the consumer and will be able to draw in more consumers.

The brand personality a marketer chooses helps create the brand. A brand needs to work on creating an identity using the visual components, such as the logo, name, colour, communication, tagline, and the experience it provides in every interface it has with the consumer. The brand personality can be youthful, fun-loving, vibrant, trustworthy, serious, having mass appeal, catering to a niche need, luxurious, and so on.

The brand building exercise takes time and consistent effort. In an ever-changing market, the consumer needs to keep pace too, and a good marketer has to stay abreast of these changes. Great brands who understand the shifting consumer pulse are able to keep their product relevant and appealing to the varying needs of the consumer.

Kotak Mahindra Bank, which had started operations in 2003, focused on investment expertise, as it had more than a decade of investment management background in its kitty. They used the tagline, 'Think Investments, Think Kotak'. With the global financial crisis altering the way financial institutes function around the world, investment banking, even at the retail level, began to get affected. Sensing the shift in consumer mood and the paradigm shift that the retail banking industry was going to be up against, Kotak carried out research, gathered feedback from its consumers, other individuals, and took a stand of its own as a bank to come up with a new brand identity with the tagline, 'Let's Make Money Simple'. The brand began to weave advertising campaigns that touched an emotional chord with the consumer and made the brand more lively and colourful. This approach helped create a new brand identity by broadening the bank's focus from investment expertise to money management support to customers in all walks of life.

Marketing is all about the strategies that a brand develops to create awareness, acquire customers, generate sales and profits. Marketing and advertising take the branding process forward by giving the required 'push' to acquire customers, drive sales and generate profits. Every communication that the brand makes with the consumer—during the sales pitch, their customer care interface, on their website, through the loyalty programme, via social media—is a part of the marketing that the brand adopts. It is every marketer's dream to have a 360-degree approach to marketing, where the brand is present on the digital platform, in print, on TV, in the outdoor medium, on social media, in below-the-line marketing. However, most brands cannot adopt this wide an approach. They need to be judicious in their chosen media for marketing as they function on limited budgets, and, moreover, the media used need to be relevant to the target audience they want to reach.

Advertising takes the communication forward and creates a connect by carrying the brand messaging to the consumer. Advertising is largely about paid campaigns. It must have the ability to get the consumer interested and then translate that into sales, thereby contributing to business profitability. The marketing team, through its marketing strategies, advertising communication and the media it chooses, must be accountable for getting the right consumers' attention and make him a customer of the brand. In today's crowded market, it is the content, its messaging, and the media chosen to reach the target audience that matter most.

Apple is a company that has achieved cult status because of the marketing strategies it has adopted. Apple is not an organisation with a marketing department that churns out strategies; rather, it is an organisation where the business is entirely focused on engaging the customer and ensuring that there is a community of customers who are the marketers of the brand. Their branding makes people desire to be associated with it, as it is not about using a computer, or an iPod or an iPhone, but about being a part of an exclusive community, which spoke about buying into a mindset. Everything about the brand, from its packaging to its clean design, is about cutting-edge technology.

The hype created around every new launch, leading to customers itching to get their hands on the product, is not just about wanting to pick up an Apple product, but about making a statement about the individuals themselves. Apple successfully lapped up technology-savvy people as its initial users who then helped build the aura the brand has created for itself.

In the early days of its inception, Apple was no different from a Blackberry or any other smart phone in the market, employing the same kind of technical experts. But they worked on creating a brilliant marketing strategy by working on the product and thereby breeding brand ambassadors out of their initial users, which led to a euphoria surrounding its products. Apple's mission was clear—to reach out to technology enthusiasts and visionaries—and they went around providing personal engravings to this fraternity, who then became the flag bearers taking the brand to the market. Similarly, they began equipping schools with iPads, and from this practice emerged an initial user fraternity who went on to get more and more people to use Apple and become a part of a cult community.

However, all this was possible only because the product strove to innovate. Apple moved away from their initial boring Apple computers by introducing colourful iMacs which became a fashion statement coupled with easy Internet access. Similarly, the iPod was a revolution in the MP3 market as it gave the option of storing 1000 songs on it as well as, with iTunes, getting songs at a fraction of the price at which a CD could be bought. The company philosophy was all about being interesting, creative, different, and getting people to adopt it and become diehard fans of its products. Apple worked on knowing the consumer and working towards giving him an experiential product that he was sure to relish.

Apple's marketing strategies provide some key insights on how a brand can create effective brand and marketing strategies. A brand strategy defines the purpose of the existence of a brand, who should communicate its brand messages, how it should work on defining itself as a brand in the minds of its target audience, where and when it should connect to its target audience and what should be its key message to its target group.

Entrepreneurs and marketers must realise that the brand strategy they adopt and the way they build it will define the success of their brand. It is critical to develop a product which has value, can build credibility, is simple to use and enhances the customer's life experiences. Once there are good products in place, the brand needs to work on creating a go-to market strategy by connecting with the consumer.

Some of the key things you need to bear in mind while designing brand strategies are:

1. **Clarity of brand purpose and creating an identity for your brand:** Have clarity as to what will be your brand purpose, what will be the differential experience your brand will offer to the consumer. In crowded markets, where there are dozens of brands which may directly or indirectly compete with your brand, it is important that you create a value proposition that is unique to your brand which will draw the consumer to your brand.

   For example, Amazon began its journey in the online e-commerce market space with the mission of wanting to be the single largest selection of products and the most customer-centric company on earth. In this endeavour, they started by building a strong digital marketing strategy by focusing on keywords and SEO marketing. Along with reaching the consumer, they focused on creating simple experiences for the consumer and used a technique of personalisation based on his buying history to make his online shopping experience delightful. Keeping in line with being the biggest selection on the planet, the company expanded by adding Amazon merchandise. Today, Amazon has millions of users spread across the globe, and they impact not only consumers but also have sellers, developers, and enterprises which partner with them to create the biggest marketplace, working together to make the customer experience better, faster, and more cost-effective.

   Along with their original purpose of wanting to provide the biggest selection, Amazon innovated to add Amazon electronic, Amazon Fashion, Amazon grocery, and also Amazon web-based services, all this in line with its mission statement of being the biggest entity focusing on the customer experience.

2. **Build your story:** In the present-day crowded market space, where your brand is competing with people in the same space as well as with products which may not be in the same space, it is important that your marketing strategy should not be about products and their features, but about how they connect with your consumer to create an emotional rapport that persuades him to be loyal to the brand on a long-term basis. Build propositions and make them the value proposition for the consumer; don't play only the price card game as that can be short-lived and you will never be able to create a differentiation with only price as the hero behind your marketing. Jio spoke about unlimited Internet access at a price advantage and that is what helped it to build a story around an IP-based technology which gives high-speed Internet access, which, in a world fuelled by rampant access to online information, was a great value proposition for consumers. And that's how it was able to bring about a revolution in terms of Internet usage in India.

3. **Be consistent:** Carefully build a brand mission and maintain consistency around core brand values, otherwise it will become difficult for the consumer to understand your brand proposition and identify with what it stands for and you will not be able to hold consumer interest. Have some core brand personality traits which could change the brand identity in the dynamic market space if consumer trends/wants/needs begin to change.

4. **Let the consumer know why:** Make your USP clear to the consumer by lucidly communicating to him across customer engagement platforms why he should pick out your brand for consumption, what value it will give him which others may be unable to do.

5. **Employees must be aware of brand proposition:** A good brand works closely with its internal clients, its employees, to ensure they know about the brand's ethos, about what the

brand is all about, and at all touch points, the team members live up to the brand identity. If your brand has a mission statement of being customer-centric, the employees need to be trained to echo that experience at every step. IBM as a company revamped the brand and built its business growth by training the entire team on ensuring that customer experience was all about customer delight.

6. **Go beyond competition:** Don't define your competition when creating your brand strategy, as this will limit the opportunities your brand will have. For example, if you are in the space of laser hair reduction, your target audience will be people who go in for waxing, and use hair removal products. Hence, you have an opportunity to compete with over-the-counter products too.

   Target non-consumers of the business too, trying to understand what keeps them away from using the category, as they will help in expanding the customer base and build better inroads into the market.

7. **Be clear on your target audience:** The power of success of a brand depends on its ability to focus and connect with its target audience. Have clarity on who form your target audience, why they will buy from you, what their age, occupation and interests are, and which advertising media they are hooked to where you can interface with them at their convenience.

8. **Brand presentation/product packaging:** The brand presentation to your target audience should resonate with what the target audience can relate to. If you are providing serious health care services, you cannot project yourself as a frivolous brand. You want your audience to connect with your brand as reliable and trustworthy caregivers offering effective treatment solutions.

Developing a brand strategy can be the vital oxygen your brand needs to grow and expand its business. The brand strategy must be built to create a brand identity which is unique, lives up to the purpose of existence of your brand, and is able to bond with the consumer through an emotional connect. It must also be consistent and create a clear picture about the brand. If a brand keeps playing with its identity and constantly changing it, consumer loyalty and repeat purchase behaviour will be weak.

A brand is all about how your consumers, your employees, your vendors view your brand, which may be a subjective perception or the hard-core reality of this image, and how through your brand strategies you will align these perceptions to your brand's purpose.

The employees are the ones who should be aligned with the brand proposition as they are the ones who breathe and live it for they create your brand with the experiences/engagement they provide to your consumers. They are the ones who will help the consumer relate with your brand proposition in all the communication, all touch points they have with the consumer.

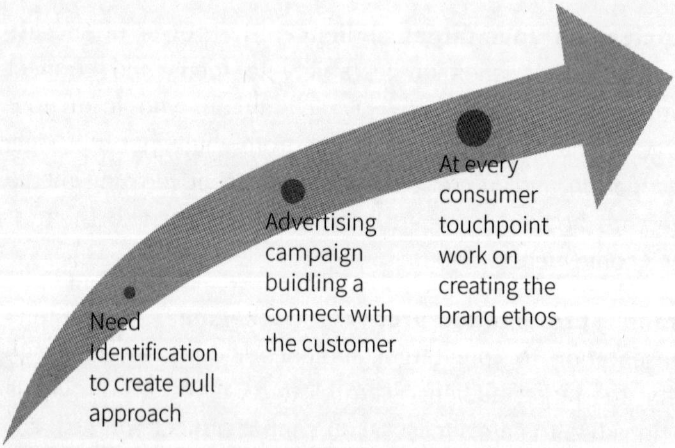

The Brand Building Mantra

4

What the Customer Needs

The consumer is the raison d'etre behind a brand. The sole reason a brand exists is that there are consumers who endorse it and use its products. If there were no consumers, there would be no brand. Hence, as an entrepreneur, it is critical for you to understand what the consumer wants and why he will keep coming to you. You need to be aware of whether your product allows you to build and maintain a relationship with the consumer, one that will keep him glued loyally to your brand. With changing times, consumer demands also change. In India, in the 1960s, right through to the 90s, the grocery market was restricted to 'kirana' shops. Each shop had its faithful chain of customers who would personally visit and buy products there.

But at the dawn of the new century, with the onset of liberalisation and the growth of the economy, people had more disposable incomes and they starting looking at better shopping experiences. Suddenly, the grocery market which had hitherto known only a few branded outlets, such as Spencer, an RPG Group company in the space of organised retail, now saw an influx of several new brands, such as Subhiksha, Nilgiris, Fabmall, Trinethra, Margin Free, and Namdhari, entered the organised supermarket space. The mall culture led to a boom in the growth of supermarkets and retail establishments, with Big Bazaar food mart, Reliance Fresh, and such brands further growing the organised retail segment. Seeing this, kirana stores too went into reinvention mode with many of them becoming air-conditioned outlets boasting of better display, visibility, and self-service options available to customers. These old-school stores understood that the consumer was increasingly conscious of hygiene and quality standards, that he was no longer content to compromise on these counts. And so the grains and groceries stocked and sold in these shops also underwent a transformation with the traditional, jute, gunny bags used for storage being replaced by handy, packaged material sealed in see-through, hygienic polybags. The billing process and the availability of trolleys and baskets for the customer to select goods intended to replicate the supermarket culture that had taken over the erstwhile shopping experience. Furthermore, the kirana stores realised that in a competitive, price-conscious market, if they were to secure a place for themselves, they would need to be more innovative and go that extra mile by doing something more. So some of them started focusing on their specific geographical connect and catering to the local needs of the customers, something that did not feature on the radar of the national supermarket stores. These revolutionised kirana stores began stocking exclusive, high-quality savouries and snacks, building a faithful clientele of customers who preferred these stores and came back for the personalised ambience offered with the convenience of being able to pick up their favourite, local savouries alongside their other daily needs. Such stores thereby created a market of consumers who were not price-conscious but, instead, were on the lookout for quality products. Kirana stores that didn't upgrade themselves lost customers, especially in the bigger cities.

Consumers have needs, and a brand must work around trying to understand what it can do to address these needs, to create a relationship with the consumer to work towards making him a loyal user of its products. Customer need analysis is the process of engaging with customers to understand their requirements for products or services and seeing how your brand can help in fulfilling these needs. Customers aren't always very clear about their needs and wants, and a good brand can help define and hone these needs. Businesses which work towards understanding their customers and creating products and services to suit the latter's needs are able to create sustainable business models.

So let's look at all the things a business needs to take into consideration about its customers:

1. **How your brand can address the customer's needs:** Customer needs are many, and knowing the ways in which you can address these by appealing to the customers is what helps a business find its connect with the consumer. For example, recent research states that being healthy figures in the top 10 priorities of people. Many brands have been working on trying to satiate the customer in fulfilling this need be healthy.

   The fitness industry has worked on creating platforms for helping the customer achieve health and fitness goals, and a plethora of brands have emerged to address these needs, right from slimming centres and gyms to weight management programmes and calorie count-conscious meal planners. Those who were able to succeed were the ones who strove to understand their customer, his lifestyle, the time he could invest, the convenience the brand could offer to gel with his current routine, and the efficiencies the brands worked on in creating effective products. Gyms came up with programmes ranging from pilates to power yoga to weight training. They took on trainers who customised the programme to suit individual member needs. This required a fair amount of discipline and motivation in implementation, and these brands worked hard to meet the needs of their consumers.

   Some brands followed the same approach blindly and launched their products. But they didn't spend time understanding how their product was faring, or what the satisfaction level was among the consumers, and that was the precise reason they failed, as they were unable to work on and develop their products around consumers' needs and they didn't take into account the latter's feedback so as to understand how to bridge the gaps between what their product or service offered and what the consumer really wanted. Brands which constantly evolve the product or service based on customer satisfaction levels are able to fare much better. This does not mean changing the product; rather, it means working on improving customer satisfaction levels through tangible as well as intangible means.

Tying up with whey protein brands, health drinks, etc., could be a collaborative advertising strategy which would help a gym to improve not only its profit margins but also public perception of being able to address all health and fitness needs under one umbrella.

2. **Unstated needs/customer delight possibilities:** Often, customers do not mention the frills and value additions, and sometimes, even the core needs that would appeal to them. If a brand is able to unravel the same through great engagement programmes and taking of feedback, it will create a set of people who become loyal users as they will feel cared for. I would like to quote the case of a Mumbai-based eatery, called Masala Library, which has outlets in Delhi as well. I remember that when the eatery opened in BKC, Mumbai, it was able to build customer goodwill because of the unique way it presented authentic Indian cuisine, combining traditional culinary skills with modern and upbeat presentation skills coupled with added elements such as palate cleansers, digestives, and ways to simply stimulate appetite so as to enable guests to experience the true flavours of the dishes. These additional touches helped to build value, as they created the USP of providing traditional Indian cuisine in a

modern manner, keeping in mind the health-conscious needs of the urban customer. This is the reason their brand stands out among the wide range of fine-dining, Indian restaurants and is a favourite of many when they want to indulge in Indian cuisine without experiencing the feeling of the food being heavy on the stomach.

3. **Clearly communicating the message:** Ensure clarity in communicating about the sales process, after-sales process, deliverables, etc. At times, caught up in the enthusiasm of buying things, customers don't pay attention to details, and a misunderstanding creeps in, resulting in customer dissatisfaction. I have come across many cases where the customer is unhappy as the sales staff as well as the buyer miss out on important communication causing customer dissatisfaction, sometimes to such an extent that the brand is left with no option but to refund the customer.

4. **Deals and offers:** Deals and offers always find a way to attract a consumer. The brand must work on targeting all type of consumers. Have you noticed that during sale season, urban malls have heavy footfall with tons of people visiting stores and often buying goods at prices that are not really all that greatly discounted. There is a rush among shoppers at such times to try and get a good deal. So a sales fest during slack periods of business will push the consumer to buy your product. But please note that if you are always discounting your products and organising sales, the consumer will accordingly build that mental image about your brand and will not make a rush towards your products.

   Many brands work innovatively to chart out a promotion strategy by setting aside those months when business is expected to be slack or the period when maximum people would want to shop as the right time for having a sale. But sales promotion may vary during both these periods, as during a slack period, discounts may be higher while during peak season, you may adopt a strategy wherein there are bonuses built in or discounts offered on picking up bigger quantities.

The discount and offer made must help the consumer to build value and perceive your brand to be good, for only then will you benefit from it in the long term. That is, businesses must work on providing quality products or perceived value-for-money products. When the AVA shops at Indian airports opened, they tied up with airlines for 'Scratch and Win' offers, wherein paying ₹750 or ₹999 was supposedly the handling charge for picking up these products. In my own experience during the initial days, I picked up three to four products, but when the quality turned out to be poor, I lost faith in them and stopped visiting the store. It is of course possible that the product quality is pretty good now, but as a consumer, the perception I built was that it's a waste to spend ₹999 on what will finally turn out to be a sub-standard product. Obviously, I am one kind of consumer; there may be other kinds of consumers who would find value in the proposition. But it is best to build a brand by making people believe in the quality you provide and not based on deals you offer.

Depending on your target audience, you may have your MRP priced at a value where the discount proposition or deals offered can be built in, without compromising on the quality of your product.

It is most important to include the cost of discounting into your projected balance sheet to understand the effect it has on your bottom line and balance sheets.

5. **Product innovation based on changing consumer needs:** The brand strategy must be flexible enough to change with shifting consumer needs. The brand ethos and brand value must remain consistent in order to maintain the brand personality.

For example, the Indian hand wash market was largely a soap market. However, with modified consumer needs of hygiene and skin care coming into the picture, brands began to reinvent the product to come up with liquid hand washes that initially targeted the upper class of society. Then slowly, with increased hygiene awareness and consumer aspirational factors awareness increased which was further enhanced with the coming up of malls and multiplexes, hand washes have become a mass product where most middle-class families use a hand wash instead of a soap. Moving your product around according to consumer aspirations and desires will always help your product stay relevant to the customer and will help you maintain or increase your market share.

6. **Decide which consumer you want to target and provide value service:** You cannot target the entire market, but you can find a segment of consumers who would be happy to use your products. If the buyer perceives value in the product, he is willing to pay the price for it. When a customer walks into a fine-dine restaurant, he does not mind shelling out the premium he has to pay for what he eats there as he perceives value in the experience, the food quality, service, and ambience. However, if the quality of any of these factors does not meet his expectations, he would not be happy shelling out the same amount and may not come back to the place again. He may even dissuade future potential customers through negative word of mouth. Hence, it is important to mindfully build the experience of the customer with the right service, food quality, and overall experience. If you walk in to Achija, a fast food joint in Ghatkopar in Mumbai, you will always find a queue there as the customer likes the food quality, the instant service at the table, and does not mind waiting for his turn as he knows he will get value for his money. On the other hand, in

a fine-dine restaurant, people expect the highest quality and instant service, are unwilling to wait for their turn, and believe in advance booking.

7. **Build care and give importance:** The customer wants to be heard and he wants to feel important. People feel pampered the minute they are given importance with a sincere greeting, instant recognition with personal mention, and warm hospitality. This will hold true for all brands. In the banking industry, relationship managers help the bank to leverage additional financial investment by taking care of the customers. In Regus, a global business leader in serviced offices, there is a standard welcome procedure with high customer service standards of delivery which ensures that the customer feels cared for. Similarly, in five-star hotels, the staff are trained to ensure the customer is always delighted, by paying attention to his particular likes and demands, and that is how they create customers who become long-term clients.

8. **A solution to the customer's problems with the right communication:** In any business, there will be times when the customer faces a problem. It is at that moment that good brands create a sustenance model for themselves by going out of the way to make the customer feel he has been heard and the solution is being worked on. It may not always be possible to resolve the customer complaint, but it is always possible to sincerely work on an alternative solution if there is no option. Never use the words—"Sorry, we can't do anything about it." Instead, change it to—"Let me see what we can do to address this."

In a highly competitive market, if a brand is not sensitive to consumer needs and wants, it will be unable to sustain its business model, however good its products are. Fiat Uno was a great car, offering good value for money, but the lack of service centres in every geography never let it achieve the status it could have had in the Indian market. We hear great stories of business turnaround that occur—all of them can be credited to focusing on the customer and his needs. Louis V Gerstner Jr transformed the fortunes of IBM when it was incurring huge losses by changing the organisational culture to one that was customer-centric. This revamped focus created IBM's historic turnaround.

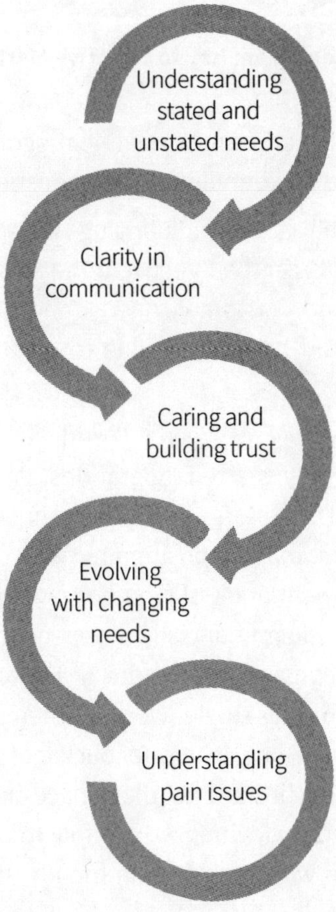

Working Towards Satiating Customer Needs

MAIN COURSE

5

Using Brand Positioning to Segment and Target the Consumer

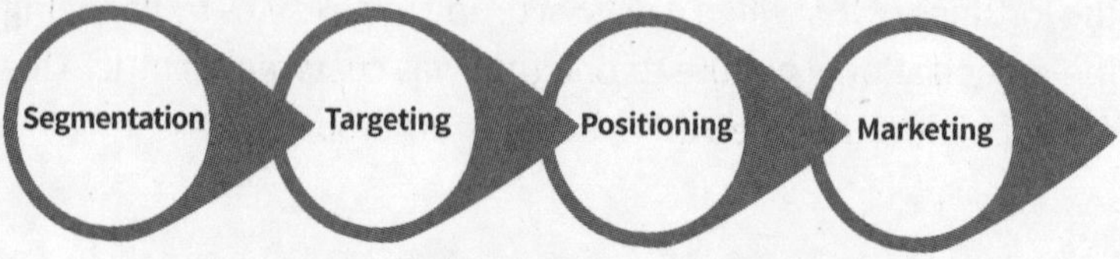

Segmentation: Key to Effective Marketing

Let us next look at the business need for segmenting the market according to brand positioning to target consumers better.

Marketing is all about influencing the consumer to buy what he needs. This can be effective if the segmentation is done well to understand customer needs and accordingly target the consumer. Good brands are able to do this based on their positioning strategy.

Let's take the case of Veena World, an all-women travel company. When they started operations in 2013, there were numerous reputed operators already in the business. Veena World adopted a brilliant market positioning wherein it realised the prevailing gap in the market of women travellers. Urban women in India were becoming financially independent and many were single. Given the conservative nature of Indian society, though, families and even the single women themselves would not be comfortable travelling in group packages where men were also present. Veena broke into that space and targeted these potential customers by inviting womenfolk to come together and let their hair down with their female friends, the company went on to provide female tour operators as guides during the trip, building a strong connect with the woman consumer. This was smart positioning for a start-up business, which soon diversified to students, honeymoon packages, grandparent packages, and today with changing customer needs, has become an affordable travel partner, moving away from its chosen original positioning which allowed it to create a footprint in the market in the first place by offering an unheard-of USP. Since the women's market was really niche, by providing the best experiential travel to this select audience, Veena World was able to capitalise its goodwill by reaching other family members and thus creating a special market for itself.

From the above example you see that the first thing a brand needs to do is to understand the kinds of consumers available in the market space, understand what their needs are all about. This is possible by segmenting the market and understanding the consumer better. In every society, consumers perceive their needs differently, which is why segmentation plays an important role as it allows you to create different communication for different people based on the segment they belong to. Segmentation can be done based on demographics, which would include parameters such as education level, income, gender, geographies, ethnicity, etc. Based on the income, education, and geography, the consumer's needs would vary. To take one example, in urban areas, where people have higher disposable incomes and their behaviour patterns do not include being very cautious in their spending habits, they would prefer watching movies at multiplexes, preferably in the luxury section. However, there is another set of people who want the experience of a multiplex but would prefer lower-priced tickets. This group would not go out during peak hours on weekends; they would instead opt for early morning shows on weekends or on weekdays, when the multiplex attracts them with better deals. This understanding of different market segments and their behaviour helps a brand achieve better occupancy and profitability. Similarly, the hotel business too segments the market and utilises the peak season to build better profitability.

Hotel rooms in luxury hotels can charge occupancy rates ranging from ₹10,000 to ₹20,000 per night during normal season, but during peak season, such as New Year's Eve, vacations, etc., the same hotel doesn't shy away from charging exorbitant rates ranging from ₹1 lakh to ₹10 lakh per night. But this is doable as consumer demand is high, and understanding the market segment that can be persuaded to buy into their deals, the hotel can play with such a variable price band. This kind of demand can be fuelled by making the customer perceive a better benefit and prestige even at the higher price.

The growth of an organisation can be steered ably if the brand understands the specific needs of various segments. In the two wheeler market, Hero Honda, apart from its presence in urban India, focused on the rural market. They built their advertising communication relevant to the rural audience wherein the consumer could relate to it, thereby allowing them to capture a major market share in rural India. As a result, their stocks have outperformed Bajaj Auto. Along the same lines, ITC and Emami, in terms of growth, are able to outperform Hindustan Lever by smartly segmenting the market and having a strong presence in rural India.

Customers or buyers are not a homogenous category; they have individual needs and it is not possible to position and create a marketing mix pandering to such individuality. But segmentation allows a marketer to create groups which have common needs and accordingly target each group by creating the right positioning and marketing mix. Segmentation is an important aspect of marketing as it helps create effective marketing strategies using relevant marketing mix based on consumer needs, thereby optimising the marketing budget and ensuring its judicious use. Segmentation would require market research and analysis of customer data.

As a marketer, it is important to understand how segmentation will enhance your productivity. The following are the key points to keep in mind:

1. It allows you to play with the price as people who are able to pay more can be tapped and price-conscious customers can also be catered to. In the multiplex example given above, we saw how a premium category in multiplexes can be created by introducing frills around the proposition, such as PVR Gold facilities, that provide for comfortably stretching while watching the movie, ensconced in a blanket, with a personal table and service rendered at the customer's table. These tactics help in tapping a segment which can pay more than others do. Similarly, the budget-conscious customer, based on his income and consumption behaviour, could be tapped leveraging a different set of ideas.

2. **Segmentation allows for building brand loyalty:** There are many brands which segment the market and have a proposition for first-time users. This is effectively used by app-based taxi services, such as Ola and Uber, who often give the first ride free, or at a discount. As the customer begins using the service, they start building loyalty by offering promotions based on usage. These promotions are largely for people who are not heavy users, until the person starts becoming loyal to the brand.

3. **Targeted communication:** Segmentation allows for targeting communication based on the segment. So, if a product has mass appeal, campaigns can be built around student offers. Think of the way Apple has effectively done this and has developed EMI (Easy Monthly Instalments) option-based marketing communication for aspirational consumers even while offering a cult, experiential, easy-use campaign for the premium category.

4. **Enhance the life cycle of the customer with your brand:** Segmentation allows for understanding the changing needs of a consumer and accordingly changing the marketing strategy and positioning your product. Retail banks work around this concept wherein they support the customer by initially offering loans and EMI options to suit his changing needs. To manage his money better, they have investment teams targeting the customers; these teams directly pitch to the customer in the capacity of relationship managers and address the need to attend to their money better.

5. **Increase market share:** Customers have diverse needs and segmentation of the market allows for increasing the market share of the brand as they are able to effectively cater to more customer segments with differentiated propositions and communication.

Once market segmentation is done, demand analysis of the various segments as it will help a brand identify the segments it will target.

It is essential to identify the right target audience where there is enough demand to help you achieve your business goals. A sample study of the target group must be conducted to understand the price point, the benefits and the kind of product that would appeal to the larger mass of this group.

To know how to be the No 1 player in the target audience that you choose, you would need to understand the segment and the different propositions that could be the drivers to create a winning proposition. This can be done by keeping the below points in mind:

1. **Does the product proposition you have created have all that this segment is looking at:** This can be understood by doing a simple survey with at least 30-50 respondents belonging to this

target group, so that the common highs in your proposition can be identified. You can hire a market research expert, or even do it on your own; the involvement and actual conversation with the consumer will help you build not only the proposition but also the marketing mix to be adopted to address this audience as you can understand the media they are exposed to on a regular basis.

2. **Understand the right target audience by grouping the users** based on age, income, gender, marital status, education behaviour patterns, any other visible trends, to see how many of them fall in your potential target group. This can be done by understanding how your product or service will help solve the problems that your proposition seeks to do. Also try to create an aspirational audience who could be attracted to your product and find out what are the common need drivers of this segment.

3. **Look at what expertise your brand can offer which will create benefit and differential need in the market for particular target audience:** Your product or service may come with some differential expertise which has a higher perceived benefit. See which target group would be able to benefit from this proposition and analyse whether the number is large enough to help you sail through in your business plan, or does your differential expertise need to be broadened based on needs and wants of other segments to create a winning proposition which will find more takers.

4. **Evaluate your competition:** See what your competitors are addressing in the target segment, what are the gaps that you can fill along with building on the product proposition you have. Evaluate and develop the USP vis. a vis. your competition, so as to really understand what will draw customers to your brand. DMart, a retail hypermarket store, worked on creating

a price advantage model where it offers branded goods at sometimes the lowest price point available in the market, but it makes up for this discounting by having a bevy of products, some of which fall under its own parent umbrella brand, which are able to chalk up high profit margins. The benefit of the best value for your money based on marketing some products is able to get the consumer to DMart. These stores always attract a high number of customers queuing up outside them. DMart, in spite of being a late entrant in the retail supermarket space, was able to build its USP on this promise of the best savings, which gave the originator of the saving revolution theme in supermarket retail, Big Bazaar, a major run for its money. DMart also targeted certain geographies, building presence in practically every part of that geography, creating pick up points by building a synergistic model of its online and offline business, thereby going beyond merely a thin presence in a city, which is another advantage and success factor for its business model.

5. **Identify the core target group:** Understand which segment which will be most excited about your product proposition as they are the ones whose problem your product proposition addresses best. This is your core group, and if you take care of it and build value additions and frills for this segment, it will help to create your first line of brand ambassadors who will become your loyal consumers and your market spokespersons who could, via prevailing social media, help build a market for you and draw other segments as well to your brand.

Based on segmentation and identification of the target audience and their needs, a brand can identify the positioning that it wants to adopt in the market. It is important to understand what positioning is all about. Positioning is the special position your brand will occupy in the mind of the consumer, relative to other, similar products available. It is all about creating the differentiators or USPs that your brand stands for, that give it a perceived position in the consumer's mind. For example, if you want your product to be positioned as a luxury product, you will have to work on the product quality to appeal to the consumer as a luxury product; the pricing of the product will also be defined in such a manner as to align it with this luxury positioning. Similarly, the product packaging and presentation must be such that the consumer finds it befitting of a luxury product tag.

In the crowded market space where competition is rampant, it is of prime importance to work on a positioning strategy. What is unique about your brand, what value proposition your brand can provide which is different from prevailing competition, how your positioning strategy will allow you to pique the interest of your target audience—these are some of the questions a brand needs to answer while working on its positioning.

As discussed above, the two key points which need to be kept in mind while coming up with the positioning strategy are:

- **Customer needs:** A good understanding of the needs of the target audience, with focus on specifics about the target group, will help design a positioning strategy which will resonate with the target audience. For example, if one was looking at starting an educational programme to upgrade the skills of working professionals, understanding the age, time availability, financial status, current professional skills and gaps based on requirements as per the industry requirements for future growth will enable you to come up with a suitable skill enhancement programme, which could offer convenience of usage and the correct value proposition to attract the audience in terms of the investment, along with having a team of faculty who could address these needs.

- **Competition:** A marketer must work on understanding what the competition prevalent in the market offers, and therefore, what is the positioning the brand will take which will help it to stand out in the market. Largely, most products offer more or less similar functional benefits, but a brand can work on creating differential advantages by working on the emotional and psychological needs of people to create a differential experience. For example, the electric vehicle market valued economy over form and function, and it had brands such as Chevrolet Volt and Toyoto Hybrids dominating it. Tesla, when it first entered the market, decided on the positioning of a luxury, high-end electric vehicle targeting a premium audience and creating specific value for it. It is best to compete on the gaps that the competition has left in the market space and has failed to serve, as this will immediately draw that audience to your brand. But you need to remember the ability of that target group to help you meet your business plan goals. There may be cases where the brand may choose a different messaging to attract another target audience.

6

Lead Generation and Customer Acquisition

Once the product and the marketing plan are ready, it is time to set the sales rolling. Sales happens when a customer pays us for the service or product we provide. Execution of the marketing plan is closely linked with sales. It starts with trying to identify who our target audience will be. This process is known as suspecting. Once the process of suspecting is complete, we need to work on finding the sales pipeline which will constitute the prospects.

The most successful people in sales are the ones who create a long and healthy sales pipeline, and this can only be achieved by meeting more and more people. I began my career as a management trainee in a paging company in 1995, when the telecom revolution had begun in India. It was my first job and I started with sales. I would immediately attend to all appointments passed by the pre-sales team. To enhance the sales pipeline, I would never miss taking referrals from the customers I created. I always had a burgeoning sales pipeline, where some customers became great professional friends who provided lots of referrals. In fact, I never shied away from having to travel two to three hours to locations in industrial areas to meet a prospect. Alongside, whenever I felt that the prospect list needed some propping up, I would readily comb different areas as a process of cold calling in the city, and this helped develop a strong sales pipeline and generate enough sales. As a result of my efforts, I became a star performer, outperforming even the dealer network in the city. Naturally, this put me in the limelight, so that in a company of over 1000 employees, the entire senior management, right from the managing director to all vertical heads, acknowledged my performance, and within six months, I was promoted. The location head of our branch in the city often teased me, saying that if I were to stand for an election, I would win hands down. I grew to be popular in the city to the extent that whenever people spoke about paging or the company I worked with, they would make a reference with the words—"the company from which that girl on the bike visited us."

I have seen that, in sales, when people fail to get results, it is because they have a limited prospect list. Even those with the most mediocre performance statistics in sales end up achieving a minimum of 20 to 30 per cent results. It is imperative for a salesperson to build a healthy sales pipeline, so that even if only 50 per cent of the prospects turn up, good results are still attainable.

So how do you create prospects to have adequate sales? Who will buy your product or service depends on two things:

1. Does the customer need or want it?
2. Are they the decision makers when it comes to buying, and do they have the ability (money) to buy it?

Even though need is the primary reason people buy, many times people buy not what they need but what they want. Take this instance. You need a TV set to watch news and entertainment channels. But when you go to a store to buy a model, you very likely buy a Smart TV, one that offers fast user interface, music streaming, video streaming, media player, universal search, and other such modern features. You may not need all the above, but you want all that in your TV and so you end up buying it. A 32-inch screen would meet your needs, but you eye a 52-inch screen and buy a 52-inch Smart TV. However, the conversion of needs or wants to sales will depend on your ability—i.e., when you have the money—to buy it.

So how does one generate a prospect list? Generation of leads is all about the right marketing coupled with the right content attracting the right audience to your product proposition. A smart marketer will evaluate available media based on the target audience along with budgets defined to make the business proposition viable and accordingly make these the channels reach the target group.

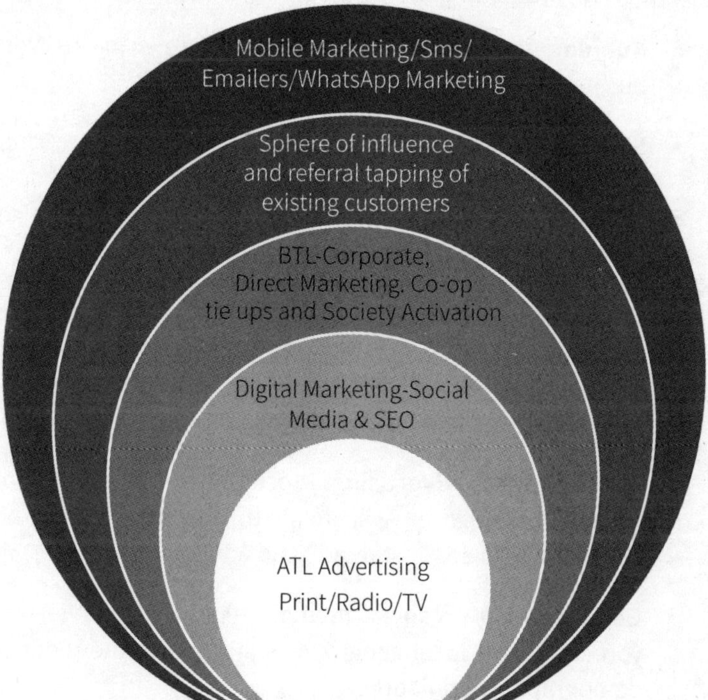

Lead Generation

Some key channels are given below:

1. **Social media, such as Facebook/Instagram marketing:** In a world that is shrinking with the advent of social media, a post that you view in one city, if it is eye-catching, is visible within hours across the entire country. An average person spends 50 minutes a day on social media, though some research

findings say that figure is higher. Most decision makers claim that they do not entertain cold calls, but when it comes to social media, they are open to conversation.

Some of the ways in which social media can be tapped effectively for lead generation are:

- **Running contests** with freebies/gifts relevant to your business to qualify the right target audience.
- **Sharing links with gated communication:** Gated communication is information that would interest people, wherein they would have to fill out basic information to get the information for free.
- **Webinars/live videos:** Live videos and webinars around your business or product will generate interest in the right target group who may then subscribe for the same, allowing you to market to that audience.
- **Social media advertising:** Social media targeting on Facebook/Instagram will help to generate leads via Facebook lead ads/Instagram lead ads.
- **Geo targeting on social media:** If your business is local, you can target local geographies along with the required demographic population.
- **Social listening:** By using search streams to monitor important keywords and handles in your industry, it is possible to uncover conversations people are having about relevant products and services, or even specific features. These people who are engaging in relevant conversation can then be reached to make a connection and share information or to create a relationship so as to persuade them to buy.

2. **SEO marketing:** Search Engine Optimisation (SEO) is the process of getting traffic directed for free to your website, blog, online content. It is an organic process where editorial and content matter enables the content to be featured on being searched. The major search engines—Google, Yahoo, and Bing—on a primary search, rank web pages and other content, such as videos, based on what they consider the user will find of value.

   The digital space in the organic world is becoming increasingly competitive and every brand needs to work on the content they share. Not only is qualitatively good content required but new content also needs to be shared on a regular basis. No single factor in SEO will guarantee high ranking. Having many links won't be of much use if they are of poor quality. Similarly, having a great HTML title won't be useful if the page has low-quality content. The website architecture should help the search engine as well as its users.

   Some useful factors involved are:

   - Quality content, which can be based on the keywords that people use in their search. When developing content, be sure to know what are the specific search words which figure in the searches people make, so that they can be incorporated in order to enable the content to figure organically, as Google, Yahoo, and Bing may perceive it to be relevant content.

   - Adding backlinks helps as it makes the content credible. (But please note that if links are of poor quality, it could backfire.)

   - **The site architecture should allow for easy, useful, and beneficial reading/visualisation:** To quote an example here, there was a website for a certain brand developed by the product's technical team which didn't work on the usage of search words which generate maximum traffic, and the site was designed blandly without keeping in mind the keyword optimisation method. As a result, the page had extremely low organic brand-building as the content was not suitably reworked by the marketing team and the digital specialist. It is imperative to understand that the consumer spends only a few seconds in today's high-content marketing world, so you should be able to draw them to your website by using keywords in headings, content and videos. Also, the content should be presented in such a way that they would want to spend time to know more about it.

- **Social media and ranking:** Likes/social signals have fast become a potential medium for ranking. Many brands work on engaging with the customer to enhance the likes and engagement platform by rolling out contests and interesting information tips.

- **Personalisation of content:** The content must be personalised and tailor-made to fit different countries and cities so as to make it relevant for users who are searching in different geographies.

3. **Referral programme:** Once you have got some customers in, you can begin working on building a referral scheme programme with aggressive monitoring of the same. The sales team needs to be trained to first collect and then convert the referrals. Top sales people always use referrals to generate new leads and broaden their sales pipeline, as a user of any product or service who has experienced the benefits, if pushed, would be more than happy to refer others to follow suit.

   Brands such as Paypal effectively used the referral method by literally giving away free money, and it worked wonders for them. This was before social media came into being. Similarly, Dropbox modelled a referral programme similar to Paypal and acquired 4 million users in 15 months.

If a referral programme is able to appeal to a consumer, it can produce phenomenal results. The Airbnb company got a single user in China who generated thousands of signups and hundreds of bookings in a single month. Amazon Prime, too, has built a successful model by using the referral programme. The best part about this method is that not only does it make the sales process and conversion easier, it also helps to get better ticket size as the consumer trusts the person referring.

4. **Corporate and society activation:** Today, corporate tie-ups have become an effective route to generating income by way of association or acquiring the leads/customers of people working in these corporates. Association with big corporates is mutually beneficial for both the new businesses as well as the established corporate houses. The latter benefit by sharpening their business proposition to their internal customers, their employees, in the dynamic market space. The new business is able to get more business and establish credibility for itself through such association.

   The healthcare segment has benefited manifold by tying up with corporate houses. The cost of acquiring a customer on the most effective medium—which is digital—varies from ₹1000 to ₹1500 in the wellness category. However, the healthcare segment has managed to make an inroad where their teams personally go to corporate houses, do activation/personal consultation for corporate employees, and are able to acquire customers at as little as one-third the digital medium cost. Corporate employees are also happy as they get service within their premises, and this in turn helps the HR team and management of the corporate to boost the organisational happiness index.

5. **Print and TV advertising:** The traditional media of advertising (print and TV) are expensive but valuable, as if you want to build the brand, print and TV foster credibility. Studies in the past clearly showed that brands which advertised in the print medium were able to generate better business and ROI (Return on Investment), but in today's evolving digital market, the personal mobile phone has become the most effective medium to know what is happening in the world as well as to find out what are the best options when looking to buy anything. Online advertising media, such as YouTube and Amazon Prime, are fast replacing print and TV as people have the freedom to stream through these channels at their convenience. Hence, there has to a right mix in the marketing plan to use print and TV platforms to enhance the brand, without missing out on creating a strong digital presence via both organic and inorganic advertising. Organic advertising is a slow process but it builds good credibility.

   Marketing budgets for a start-up should never be on the higher side. They will vary from business to business. A new business must adopt what Jay Conrad Levinson in his book *Guerrilla Marketing* calls "cost-efficient marketing methods". Ideally, a budget for a new business should be planned minutely with the top line required. It should never be more than 10 per cent of the gross sales. B2B businesses would require a much lower marketing budget.

6. **PR (Public Relations):** PR is an effective medium to create buzz in the market about the launch of a product or service. It also involves lower costs compared to print and TV advertising. Many big brands were launched via PR, including Facebook, Google, Twitter. Mark Zuckerberg launched Facebook at Harvard in 2004. After its rapid growth, with 90 per cent of Harvard students using it, he moved on to eight universities

in the Ivy League. And thereon, to all graduates. It was only in 2007 that through a PR release, Facebook was launched with the headline, 'Facebook Goes Off the Campus'. Today, the social media giant is worth billions on the stock market.

Moreover, in the digital medium, PR can be done effectively by using influencers and bloggers. Many start-ups let leading influencers and bloggers experience their products and services so that they can build interest among their followers for the same.

7. **SMS/email marketing:** Text messaging, according to Nielsen, is the most common data service in the world. It has the advantage of being instant—93 per cent of texts are opened within three minutes—thereby offering one of the best ways to connect with the consumer. Considering the competitive edge that text messaging offers, you can use it for your brand thus:

   - Your web pages, such as Facebook, websites, or any other online platform, must prominently display the text number. A lot of people surf the Internet during the night. Hence, they may prefer to leave a text message rather than make a call.
   - Offer deals on texting to generate call-to-action leads.
   - Texting can be used as a vital customer service tool, allowing you to revert promptly, which would create an experience of great, timely customer response.
   - Feedback/reviews are a good way to engage customers and create upselling opportunities.

   Email marketing is not intrusive and it offers people the comfort of having a look at leisure. If the content/headline are good, if they are inviting enough, chances are the consumer will open them. Research states that $1 invested in email marketing still yields returns worth roughly $44.25.

No doubt, email marketing has to be attractive and engaging, and it has to cater to people at various phases of the buying cycle. Artificial Intelligence (AI) and predictive analysis are great ways to tap customers effectively. Many organisations do not use the CRM tool to engage customers efficiently. If, from day one, you devise a system that maps the customer cycle and you review and set engagement platforms at various buying cycles, you will be able to create better ROI per customer. In many instances, brands collect leads but these leads are not tapped effectively. Therefore, software integration and review lets you build a system that plugs the loops in the lead drop and maps lead generation effectiveness too.

The next question that arises is how the email should be designed to be able to generate effective leads.

- The subject line must compel a consumer to open the email. For this, it is important to understand the core need that is going to drive the consumer to use your product or service. This will not only generate interest but also qualify the lead.

- The imagery must reinforce the message you are trying to communicate as the human brain comprehends visual imaging first.

- Too much text in the communication can lead to drop out while reading the email. Make available bullet-pointed communication interwoven with links so that people can click on these links to get more detailed information.

- **Social platforms:** In the age of social media, it would make sense to give users the option to share your email communication across platforms such as Facebook, LinkedIn, Twitter.

they are most likely to produce results. Here, there is also greater ease and accuracy in measuring results. The medium used are telephone, mail, telemarketing, voice marketing, and door-to-door selling.

Eureka Forbes pioneered direct marketing by knocking on doors of the common masses. When the vacuum cleaner was launched in the Indian market at ₹30,000, people were unconvinced as to how it could possibly substitute a broom costing just ₹10. But through direct marketing and one-to-one education, a market for vacuum cleaners was created. Initially, the team would just knock on doors and approach people with their products, but to suit today's times, with the salesperson unable to make it past the watchman for security reasons, the company reinvented and created a model of digital awareness and appointments clubbed with direct marketing, whereby the salespeople began visiting the customer based on prior appointments.

12. **Inbound marketing:** This is one of the most effective lead generation techniques as the relevant target audience is drawn to the website by the right and meaningful content. The opportunity to convert, close, and delight the consumer is humongous, as it leverages on the strength of all the other marketing/lead generation measures that a brand takes. Inbound marketing is effective as it can be mapped and productivity can be gauged by using an effective CRM tool. Moreover, the chances of educating the customer to buy your product is higher, while relevant communication will make him spend more time and thereby convert. The best part is that it is a cost-effective medium that avoids wastage of other marketing/lead generation strategies your brand adopts and thereby helps create qualified leads.

Lead generation is one of the most critical parts of a business cycle as it forms the foundation for getting in customers. Many organisations work in a haphazard manner, reminding me of a man racing through the garden trying to catch butterflies with a net who does not manage to catch even one. It is imperative that a proper strategy should be devised to work on lead generation, keeping in mind the business plan, the budget available, and required leads to achieve the business objectives. Since it would require experience, talent, and exposure to successfully generate leads, you need to carefully evaluate the option of either doing lead generation in-house or outsourcing it to experts who have had definite success in the past. If you have a good team which understands all the platforms you want to tap, then it may be a good idea to do it in-house. There could also be a synergistic approach adopted, whereby you work on some platforms in-house where the team is strong and work with partners where there are internal gaps.

Start-ups must focus on cost-effective ways, and innovatively work out an initial plan to draw in leads without going beyond the budget. This would involve a plan that combines an online awareness action campaign along with an on-ground activation programme to drive in leads.

7

Sales Pitch

Once you have the leads flowing, it is time to start converting. The word 'sales' is not always seen in a good light. Many don't like being called 'sales people'. I must share an incident I personally encountered.

I was engaged, and my wedding date was fixed. My to-be mother-in-law went to invite one of her neighbours for our big fat Indian wedding that was two months away. It so happened that the daughter of that family was working in the customer care department of the company I worked with. Even though she had never met me, as I was posted in a different location, she had heard about me. When she heard that I was the bride, a sales person in her company, she made a face and said in a derogatory tone, "Oh! She is in sales."

One day, after I was married, my in-laws wanted to know more about what was this sales profile I was employed in, and whether it was respectable.

I have learnt from experience that being in sales and subsequently handling marketing is purely what gave me an edge in my career, because it was that arm of the business that brought revenue to the organisation. Sales results always spoke about performance in black and white. Furthermore, what one learns in a sales career plays a significant role in shaping a person professionally much better, as it teaches one the art of dealing with different kinds of people and develops the faculty of emotional intelligence.

Actually, if you think about it, sales is something all human beings are constantly practising right from a very early age, from the time they become aware about themselves and the world around them. A child wants attention, and learns to sell antics and tantrums to get it. When children go to school, the smarter ones learn to sell their behaviour and persona to the teacher in such a manner that the latter starts paying particular attention to them. As children make friends, they start pitching their fun-loving personality so that they are able to gather more friends around themselves.

Therefore, although technically, the word 'sales' can't be applied in the above situations, where there is no transaction of financial nature between two parties in return for goods or services taken, it is correct to say that an individual is constantly achieving what he or she wants by 'selling' something or the other.

Sales is an inherent aspect of every successful person's personality. In every organisation, I have seen how people who aren't directly involved in the sales function are constantly building their credibility by selling the work they are doing. They keep letting people around them, especially the bosses, know about all they have done and are doing. To be successful, one needs to know the art of selling. But the important question is this: *Is sales an art that only some people can be good at?*

The answer is that sales is both a scientific process and an art, as it requires one to master the art of communicating effectively as per the scientific sales process laid down in order to build trust. Trust is the prerequisite for any sales to materialise. Sales is all about touching the emotional chord with a consumer, for emotions are what open the cheque book.

Let me recount here a personal experience that shows how emotions can play a big role in driving sales. My son was one year old, when an acquaintance who was in multi-level marketing introduced me to Lotus Books in the late 1990s. She showed me a series titled *Early World of Learning*, and explained to me how effective it was in building a child's learning skills. I went ahead and invested about ₹12000 to place an order. For a parent, there could be nothing more important than providing the child with all the right learning tools. Let me tell you that this amount I shelled out was almost 75 per cent of the monthly salary I was drawing then. The delay in delivery of the books led me to meet this acquaintance's upline contact (the manager). He was a retired Air Force officer and the most effective salesperson I ever met. He began visiting us and steadily built an emotional rapport, at first talking about how my son, Saurabh, would become a genius. He introduced me to the world of bindi (round, colourful accessory) counting, telling me that Saurabh could become a mathematical genius like Shakuntala Devi. I believed everything he said. He casually shared a poem about a mother-and-child relationship, one that instantly struck an emotional chord. As a young working mother, his words evoked all my emotions, making me want all the more to give the best to my child. I had tears in my eyes on reading the poem. I ended up buying another two sets of books, worth ₹ 40000 approximately, for a child who was not even one-and-a-half years old at the time. If I told you that a one-year-old child who could not read alphabets began to recognise words, most people would not believe it. I bought into everything that manager said and found it acceptable to spend so much money on buying those books. Even though my son didn't know how to read the alphabet or put together letters to make words, my belief in the sales pitch led me to perceive that my toddler could read words, including big words such as 'elephant'. When I began showing him words such as 'elephant' written with the letters and kept stating that it was an elephant, he actually began reading that spelling as a pictorial word meaning elephant in his mind. Today, I know that my child was introduced to the spelling via the pictorial representation of an elephant, and it was a method of pictorial learning for him.

I never repented buying those books, as they helped foster my child's early learning skills. Those books were part of the reason why he grew to be a voracious reader at a time when most children were not reading books at all, and there's no doubt that reading helped shape his personality. But the point I am trying to emphasise here is that emotions usually open the purse and result in sales.

Sales is the key driver to revenue which keeps an organisation afloat. Hence, the entrepreneur must build an effective sales team where the right processes are set down early on. Review and monitoring of sales must happen on a regular basis. The entrepreneur must always keep a tab on the top line as well as the bottom line—the two facets of business profitability.

Let us familiarise ourselves next with the sales process. The sales and marketing process begins with suspecting who the customer is. Once that is done, we begin prospecting to this audience.

The customer has needs and the product/service provider wants him to consume their products/services. However, there are gaps between what the consumer wants and what the sales person pitches. An effective sales process is one that tries to close these gaps.

Which is why, I give the acronym 'GAP CLOSE' to the sales process, which is defined as below:

Greeting by introducing yourself

Ascertaining customer need and building a rapport

Pitching your product and introducing your company

Consensus building as per needs cited by the customer

Leading to a close

Objection handling

Sale closure by looking at closing cues

Evolving a relationship via feedback and setting up a post-sales follow-up process

1. **Greeting by introducing yourself:** Breaking the ice with the customer sets the right tone for the meeting, keeping

in mind the relevance of the conversation and the time the person has to give you to pitch the product. We can always begin with a line complimenting the customer, his brand, or his office. However, this must be a genuine compliment. Do not give a personal compliment to a prospect as you do not know the person on a personal level and you do not know what could disturb the equilibrium. A general statement along the lines of—"Thank you for giving me time at such short notice. It is a pleasure to meet you. I must say your brand has made great inroads in the market space..."—could be an approach you adopt.

Your approach has to be warm, smiling, courteous and caring. It is said that the first five minutes of interaction define your ability to connect with people. If you are able to create an impact at that time, you will get the person interested in listening to you. There are some important factors when it comes to creating a first impression, as it will set the tone of your meeting.

Let's take a look at some of the things a sales person has to bear in mind before he goes for a sales call.

- Being well-dressed with clean, hygienic looks
- Being well-groomed. Girls must wear basic makeup, have their hair neatly tied
- Men must have clear nails, be clean shaven, or have a well-maintained beard, wear polished shoes
- Smiling warm demeanour
- Punctuality in keeping the appointment, respecting the other individual's time
- Eye contact with confident approach
- Being well-prepared with all required sales tools, brochures, visiting card, presentation, calculator, etc.

2. **Ascertaining customer need and building a rapport:** Understand the customer better and develop a rapport based on their underlying needs/desires which your product will be able to address. The best way to do this is to ask open-ended questions to understand three things:

   - **What does the customer want:** If you can gauge what it is that the customer is looking for in the product/service, you make a note of the same and customise your pitch accordingly while presenting the product/service. If the customer sees that all that he wants is available in what you are offering, that eases consensus building when you are pitching the product, making it easy to lead the sale to a closure. For example, someone planning to buy a new mobile phone may be looking for a good quality camera, good battery life lasting 24 hours, multimedia phone Bluetooth, good memory/storage of 32 GB or 64 GB, all within a budget of say, ₹30,000 to ₹40,000. If you understand these parameters early on, it will be extremely easy to bring the product sale to a closure quickly as the customer will see that you are able to fulfil most of his wants.

   - **The problem with most sales people** is that they are too keen on closing the sale and, in the process, they do not comprehensively understand all that the customer wants. They are entirely focused on pitching the product as soon as possible. What the customer needs and what the sales person offers do not match, and this gap raises objections and the sale does not fructify. Can a doctor prescribe a medicine without fully understanding the symptoms of the patients? If a sales person is able to get an understanding of the 'what', i.e., what the consumer wants to buy or the perception of the customer regarding the product, the sale closure will always be higher than the current closure.

- **Why does the customer want it?:** Examining the 'why' behind customer needs will aid in carrying out benefit analysis. Sometimes, consumers themselves are not clear about their needs, and asking questions that reveal why they want what they want will bring clarity to their mind as well as equip the sales person to pitch the product according to what the consumer perceives as benefits he will avail of. Commitment building in a good sale closure happens through this process. However, one has to be careful about the way the 'why' question is posed, as some customers may not be open to answering the question if it sounds inappropriate in any way to them. An ideal way to ask this kind of question is—"Sir/Madam, what are the benefits you are looking for in this product/service?" Let's look at the case of a person who wants to buy a house. If we put to him a summarised statement after understanding his basic needs, we will be able to build commitment.

- "I understand you are looking at a 2BHK (Bedroom, Hall, Kitchen), garden facing, with an east-west view, having amenities including a swimming pool, gym and club house, in the central suburbs of Mumbai. That way, you will be able to provide your children with a place where they can enjoy all-round personality development. Is there anything else that drives this decision? If you let me know, I could explore options to look at meeting those requirements as well."

- Asking questions in this manner makes people comfortable to discuss their needs better and takes it to a closure.

- When does the customer want it: The timeline of the customer's purchase will give you a good understanding as to whether the lead is warm/cold/hot. But one can't ask a point-blank question—"When are you looking at buying?"—except in the sale of a high-value item, such as a house/office space/holiday trip. For products that are not high-value items, you need to lead it to a closure by making statements along the lines of "We could provide delivery for this today," and see how they respond. Or, we could say, "Sir, would you prefer to shift in this month, or will next month also do for you?" (if the discussion is about a house). If the customer is a fence sitter, a sales person can use an offer pitch for immediate closure, or closure within a week, thereby transforming the customer into a hot lead.

3. **Pitching your product and introducing your company:** Once the customer's needs are understood, the sales person can go ahead and introduce his company or brand. The brand value must have a uniqueness (the USP of the brand) that should be the clear differentiation point in a competitive market, which makes the customer find value in the brand proposition.

   Here I would like to quote a relevant example of how brands can be created and how they work in a market. In the serviced office space, Regus was the global leader. A team of 12 Regus employees went ahead and joined a UK-based group called Avanta, a small brand that had made its first foray into an international market in India. But the sales team there went ahead and built a positioning that claimed Avanta was a premium business centre with high-end service quality, which the operation team lived up to. In such a scenario, Avanta was able to capture great market share even in a recession-driven market.

4. **Consensus building as per needs cited by the customer:** This is the most important part of the sales process, because after introducing the company/product/service, the pitching must be done keeping in mind the needs identified in Step 2 of the sales process. If this consensus building while pitching

the solution to customer needs is done, agreement building with the customer falls in place, and he is oriented faster towards understanding how the product/service will meet his needs. The sales person needs to keep in mind the what, why and when behind customer wants, so as to smoothen the sales process. When a customer is buying, he needs to understand the benefits he will accrue. Many sales people keep their pitch restricted to product features only, where relating to the features becomes difficult for the customer and value for the product/service is not built. If the same proposition is built on pitching the product/service as per needs and benefits that the customer is looking forward to, the latter will be open to a sales closure.

For example, if in the case of a customer looking to buy a 2BHK house, the sales pitch states, "I have just the right house as per your requirements. It is a spacious 2BHK overlooking the best garden view which will help you and your family enjoy the greenery as well as keep an eye on your children when they play in the garden. The swimming pool is also located nearby just as you wanted. The best thing about the house is that it is extremely auspicious, as it meets your needs of east-west opening. You will always have fresh air in the house because of the western wind flow, ensuring healthy and comfortable living. What do you think, will this be the right option to look at?"

Consensus building or commitment building as per customer needs should be the key pitch to generate customer identification with what he needs.

5. **Leading to a close:** Most customers actually don't buy what they need; they end up buying what they want. The want is what the customer identifies in the 'why' underlying his needs. This can be built on the aspirational needs of a consumer.

But one needs to understand that, in the process, the ability to buy should not be lost, as there are times that a customer aspires to buy something better but he does not have the ability to do so. When he has the ability to buy it, the want becomes a demand. A sales person has the ability to convert a want into a demand, by creating value for the product.

Let's take the example of the iPhone when it first wanted to tap the Indian market. At that time, the market was dominated by good phones costing less than ₹20,000. The iPhone was perceived as a premium aspirational product which many people found to be just a want. Apple came up with a brilliant sales and marketing strategy of EMI options requiring a payment of a nominal ₹6000 to ₹8000 per month. Suddenly, the market experienced a jump and the iPhone went from negligible market share to capturing 4 per cent, owing to a marketing strategy that appealed to the price-conscious, aspirational Indian consumer.

Similarly, the SUV market in India grew exponentially by pitching the right value proposition of getting families together on the diverse Indian terrain. All brands realised that there is a market for SUVs, and in the last decade, the market has seen a plethora of SUVs being launched. The SUV market grew by approximately 21 per cent in 2018, compared to passenger cars which grew by just over 3 per cent. The hatchback and sedan markets were overpowered by SUVs based on the sales and marketing pitch adopted.

6. **Objection handling:** The reason why people don't buy is that they perceive a gap between what they want and what is offered to them. Hence, as a good sales person, you must judiciously use consensus building questions while pitching the product/service. During the sales pitch process, keep leading the customer to come to a closing sentence. Whenever

you try that, you will realise that if the customer is not moving to a closure, there is surely an objection at play that is holding him back.

Let's take a look at the earlier example of a customer who has come to buy a 2BHK house. After we have got the answer to the question of whether it is the right house for the customer, we can start leading to closure by engaging in objection handling. The next question could be, "So which of these bedrooms would you choose for yourself?" Or "I can customise the bathroom tiles as per your taste, would you want to customise one bathroom or both?" If he answers in the affirmative, you know that he is giving you a signal for closure. If not, you lead him to another closure sentence, such as, "So are you looking at a professional interior designer, or would you prefer to do the interiors yourself?"

After every objection you handle, after every leading question, pitch a close-ended question with two options. (Close-ended questions are those which give two options, out of which the customer will ideally pick one option, whereas an open-ended question is one where you ask a question and a customer can answer anything. Open-ended questions are asked during the probing stage when one is trying to understand customer needs.)

Never ask an open-ended question once you are trying to close the sale. Your next question could lead to a sales closure. For instance, you could ask, "I have the same option on Floor 2 which is priced at 1 crore, and Floor 7 which is priced at 1.15 crore, because of the floor height increase and better view. Should I book the second floor for you, or would you prefer to take the seventh floor house?"

This is a definite sale-asking/closure-asking question. Once you have asked this kind of question, please wait for an answer and do not say anything. If the customer does not answer, you may repeat the question. If his answer is in the negative, then you need to note that he still has some objections to the buying and you need to address these. As a sales person, you can always evaluate if there is an option that will make sense to your consumer based on his objections. When you do that, the chances of your closing the sale are much higher.

7. **Sale closure by looking at closing cues:** When a customer is addressing an objection, it is a sign that he is interested. If he wasn't, he wouldn't spend time talking to you. There will, of course, be some rare exceptions. If a customer leans forward, looking at the floor plan, or takes out his spectacles or a calculator, or asks for financing options available, he is telling you he is ready for the sale to be closed. Don't deviate at that point and do ask for the sale. Soft selling is the right way to go forward while closing a sale. To close the sale, you should put to the customer a close-ended statement, such as, "I am blocking the second floor for you." Wait for an answer, then ask, "So will you pay the booking amount of ₹50,000 by cheque, or would you prefer to make a card payment now?"

   If the customer does not buy, there is still something that is holding him back. Try to understand that through objection handling again, without sounding pushy. If a customer is spending time trying to understand your product/service, he is a potential buyer, and how you handle him in trying to understand his needs and building consensus while pitching your product will be the key to bagging the sale. However, if the customer needs time as his finances are not in place, or if immediate requirement is not there and it is only a future need he is exploring, clarification of his needs and building commitment will encourage the customer to come back to buy from you in the future.

If gaps in your product/service are the reason for deferment of decision by the customer, work within your organisation to see if it is possible to address that issue. Especially if it is becoming a generic issue for many consumers who are not buying, that means the customer is giving you a sure signal that he needs to buy but these are the gaps you must fill in first.

8. **Evolving a relationship via feedback and setting up a post-sales follow up process:** To create happy customers who build your brand and generate referral for you, it is important to make clear the post-sales process. The documentation to be done, the warranty offer, the after-sales service, the special benefits you are offering to someone when they become a customer, the customer service helpline, and your contact number—these are vital details you must share with the customer.

   Never forget to ask, "Is there anything else you want to know? Please feel free to get in touch with me if there is anything else you need." And if they call you first, be ready to help. Good customer service will help you garner goodwill from the customer and, in the process, get referrals.

   Feedback taking is a great tool to help you understand if there is anything you need to work on to up your skills and take better care of your customer. Happy customers create a successful brand. A brand which does not understand the gaps in their customer experience and doesn't work on feedback taking will lose market share in a competitive market.

   Let me share the experience of car servicing. I personally went to collect my car after a servicing session. The service executive handed me a feedback form and I rated the overall experience as 9 on a scale of 10, with 10 being the highest rating. The executive asked me, "Why not 10, Ma'am?" My husband in his usual direct manner stated, "Because that's what we feel about your service station." I added that 9 is a very decent rating. The executive then tried his best to ask what they can do better, and in fact, he got his manager to join the discussion. My husband said that the ambience could definitely do with a revamp, and I added the fact that it was too much of a hassle to come and drop the car and then come back to pick it up later. I loved the way he took our feedback and turned around and said, "We will definitely work on your feedback and we shall offer you a free pick up and drop the next time you want your car serviced." His response addressed my problem and also made it possible to satisfy my expectations of having someone take the car for servicing and drop it back once it was done. This was easier for him to do than to change the interiors of his service centre.

The only way a brand can improve is by understanding where there are gaps that need plugging. People who constantly do this are able to create more customer-friendly brands by working with simple, realistic solutions to address customer happiness and make the customer experience a delightful one.

It is important, though, to take the feedback on a digitalised platform so that the managers/supervisors/leadership team can discuss and come up with plausible solutions.

During a discussion on customer delight, I remembered an incident that a colleague narrated about his roommate who worked in a five-star hotel. He mentioned how every Friday, after a late shift in the hotel, his roommate would pore over his diary, looking at customer issues raised and their solutions implemented because he would have a meeting with the general manager of the hotel the next day. Having such a strict review system likely helped the five-star establishment build its reputation and live up to the high standards ensuring that their customers were always delighted.

Asking for referrals is the best way to build new prospects as happy customers will drive other people to your brand. But it makes more sense to go ahead and ask for referrals. A good sales person is always able to perform better as, at any given point of time, he has a pipeline of new prospects. This is thanks to the relationship he builds with people whom he sells to, who are always happy then to recommend the business to their family and friends.

I personally was able to do better than most colleagues in sales as I was always hungry for more sale and would constantly look at new ways to get business. The only reason my pipeline kept growing was because I would not forget to take referrals. I would diligently make general follow-up calls too to generate new referrals from old customers, and they would rarely disappoint me. Obviously, there were times they couldn't think of any more names to refer, but my persistence would pay off some other time as I would get a call from them whenever they were sitting with a friend who was looking at the same product. I never let happy customers forget me, and they never forgot me and my brand because of my persistence.

It is necessary to be aware that sales does not always happen in just one pitch; there is a lot of persistence that goes into the process. There are some sales pitches where you need to follow up with the customer many times. Most people buy when a person persistently follows up with them. But that does not mean one should become a pest that people dread. Sales is relationship selling. You must respect people, their time, and be at the top of your soft sales pitch. A few days ago, I got an email from a person who wanted to pitch his business analytical solution to my brand. There are many people who approach me via email/social media. But the way he drafted his email made me take note of it and I fixed a meeting with him. His note stated, "I understand you are extremely busy and I don't want to sound like a nagging pest as this is my third email to you, but I have an excellent solution for your organisation and I am confident that it would be worth your time."

Persistence combined with respect for other people's work and time will definitely open a door for you to approach them, and if you are good enough and have worked sincerely to create a great solution for people, they will buy from you.

When I worked with a media house that was the Number 2 player in the market, there was a huge gap in market share between the market leader and us. We had to keep creating value additions, whereby we added offline events and digital platforms to create a value proposition that would make sense to the advertiser. This helped us get more business. We also had to constantly innovate and maintain a persistent approach to help the advertiser understand the value proposition we would provide. This approach helped us crack many accounts which had never before advertised with us.

Insurance sales is built largely on relationship building. All the insurance products I have bought have been a direct outcome of the persistence levels of the individuals who approached me or the personal equation I enjoyed with these people.

If you want your product to do well in the market, you need to hire and train a team which understands soft skills, is passionate about their work, and is willing to move around honestly to generate business. New business is dependent upon the number of new prospects we add and how happy our old customers are with us.

Moreover, the quality of the sales team you hire will be critical in building your business. It is better to hire one good person than two, as the success of a new product will be dependent on the productivity of you and your team. Create good monitoring systems and set the right expectations with people to get the best out of them.

The Sales Process

Need Analysis: Probing and building consensus by understanding and citing the need

If need understood, then go to ↓

Pitching the Product: Talking about benefits and relating them to consensus built, so that product matching with need done

If No, Repeat. *If matching consensus built, then go to* ↓

Objection Handling: Cite The Objections And Remove Them By Reasoning And Probing

If No, Repeat. *If objections removed, proceed to* ↓

Proceed with pitching the close, looking at closing cues. If no cues, then probe into pitch closure

If customer is positive with closure pitched, then ↓

Ask for sale

Collect money and proceed to ↓

Take feedback and build long-term relationship

8

PEOPLE MANAGEMENT

It is rightly said that people make an organisation. An organisation's success or failure depends on the people working in it for it is they who drive it, and it is the culture they create that makes or breaks the company. Therefore, it is important to set the right expectations with people and to have them aligned with the company goal. How does one do that?

First and foremost, people need to feel that they belong to an organisation, they should feel important and proud to be a part of it. This requires an organisation to have identified unique achievements which employees can relate to and feel proud of. When the marketing team works on building the brand, it is the internal consumer—the employees—who play the most important role. If the employees start believing in the organisation's mission and vision statement and understand what their brand stands for, they will start breathing life into the brand at every consumer connect, living up to the brand vision.

Even an excellent business model, if not backed by the right HR policies, would see the organisation lose good people and, in the process, see the business going downhill. I used to work with a global real estate group which was the leader in its category, and they had one of the most amazing business models in the market with outstanding business margins, especially in the Indian market. They had excellent SOPs with streamlined sales processes, aggressive induction programmes in the global market on sales training and processes. However, when they launched their Indian operations, they were unable to build a strong HR framework. I saw many cases of people who couldn't be aligned with the company goals, and a large chunk of good talent left the group. Most employees didn't feel any sense of job satisfaction while working there. In fact, a time came when quite a few people from senior and middle management to junior staff levels went on to join a competitive group. The new group was built on a poor business model with low business margins and failed to sustain their business operations for more than a year. When the international arm of the new group decided to sell their Indian arm to the global business leader, not even a single employee decided to continue being a part of the global leader, even though none of them had a job in hand anymore because of the sudden takeover. This case clearly demonstrated that the right kind of HR engagement is critical to sustenance of the business.

Communication and trust are the foundation of the edifice for a good brand to be created. Constant engagement with people is immensely important for the business. When running an organisation, if you think about who are the people whom you would call the 'top performers' or the most committed ones, you will find it is those whom you engage with the most. Involving people makes them feel wanted and, in turn, they feel motivated to deliver.

I have had the opportunity to see first-hand how good HR policy and engagement can take an organisation's performance to the next level. I joined a Swedish multi-level marketing company as manager for one of their branches. Initially, I was functioning on my own, with limited access to the head office for approvals and other basic information. With a change in the leadership, we were called to the head office every month, which put us in alignment with the company goals, sharing best practices and creating healthy competition among the branches. The new country head also convened the national staff gathering, where every employee was called in and engaged in a two-day programme. This helped us relate to being part of a common vision and goal, allowing to create teams that were competitive, productive, and in sync with the company goals. Within a short period of time a 30-crore business (nationally) grew manifold, to about five times what it had been. Today, the same company is a 1000-crore business in India.

Circuit City, an electronics store in the US, which scaled from a level of mediocrity to excellence, believed in getting the right talent on board. When Vice President Walter Bruckart was interviewed on what were the top five reasons that led to this transition, he said, "One would be people, two would be people, three would be people, four would be people, and five would be people." He firmly believed that this transition was possible only because of their discipline to pick the right people who were able to leverage the brand to the next level.

So, the next question is, how does one engage the right people?

People innately need to feel important and valued. If you look back at your school days and think about which class you enjoyed the most, it will probably be the class where the teacher interacted with you maximum and appreciated you. As a result, you developed a liking for that subject and gave your best in it. Similarly, in an organisation too, one enjoys the job when the management/manager acknowledges the work, appreciates it when employees put in effort, and creates platforms for people to excel and showcase their work. Everyone wants success, money and fame, but how many really strive to achieve what they want. There are mainly two kinds of people in any organisation. One, those who are self-driven performers—such people require appreciation/acknowledgement via engagement and a clear path for growth. Two, the majority of employees—who are part of the system but need to be constantly monitored with expectation-setting, who need to be driven so as to help them realise their personal and professional goals.

How can a growing organisation ensure that every employee who joins the group is truly involved?

This would require extensive training and monitoring as well as fostering a culture of accountability. An organisation needs to work on the middle management extensively, by making them understand the most important dynamics of success in life. Managers alone can do only a limited amount of work; if they are to be successful, they need to nurture a competent team under them who will shoulder the responsibility of ensuring timely completion of tasks. Many managers fail to realise that they can climb to the next level only if they train others who can fit into their shoes. I have seen some managers who believe they have to do everything themselves. In the process, they only limit their success, as they certainly can't be omnipresent and they are unable to raise others to a level where they can carry out tasks to perfect completion even in the absence of the managers. During my stint with Oriflame, a multi-level marketing Swedish group, as branch manager, when my customer service team was called to the head office, they fared much better than the other customer service teams. They knew the sales plan explanation like the back of their hand, and they were well aware of the targets and achievements of the branch even though their job was largely restricted to billing and addressing issues that cropped up while billing. On returning from the head office meet, they proudly told me that they were really appreciated there, and it spoke volumes about my management style. I have always believed that you cannot do a task alone; your entire team needs to be in sync and competent enough to handle the work.

Moreover, people need to be reviewed constantly, for even the best of people tend to slacken if their work is not monitored. Reviewing work helps to set expectations. However, it must always involve three ways of giving feedback.

The first encompasses all the things that the individual is doing well and all that they need to further work on. Constantly pointing fingers only makes people defensive and hinders productivity. However, that does not mean that shoddiness in timely delivery of work can be taken leniently. One needs to create a culture of accountability where people need to fall in line with organisational goals, and the importance of their professionalism as also the key result areas of performance required of them need to be explained to them.

Secondly, work with people to help them grow and thereby help yourself grow too. To quote from my own example, I had joined a media house with no experience in the field. My supervisors were apprehensive as to whether I would be competent in my work. At one point, three new management trainees having more or less the same calibre joined, and one of them was in my team. When their work was reviewed, the lady who was working with me fared much better than the others because of the effort I had invested in working with her. This developed confidence in my supervisor regarding my work.

Thirdly, communication flow must be clear and transparent. Lack of communication creates distrust and subsequently misunderstandings, which results in derailment of people from work goals and loss of productivity.

People also look at work-life balance. I have many friends who work at a software arm of the Tata group, which has great HR practices, flexible work hours, work-from-home options, and even crèches available for their kids. Some of my friends who got placed in this group have stuck with it through thick and thin, their career now spanning over 20 years, thanks to the excellent support they got that enabled them to manage both work and home fronts, along with opportunities to be recognised for their work.

The right HR policy is all about 'RESPECT'. I use the word here as an acronym for a set of factors that play a key role in shaping progress in every business. So, if an organisation gives RESPECT to its employees, the trained employees are retained for longer tenure, and subsequently, driven employees steer the company forward on the road to success.

Here is what 'RESPECT' for employees as part of HR jargon means:

R for Recognition, value and respect—People like to be recognised and valued for their work. They need to know that they are cherished stakeholders. This is possible only when their opinions are valued and recognised and they feel an overall sense of being respected. Many people, when they feel valued, don't mind working at pay packages which are not the most competitive in the market. Respect for employees helps them feel cared for as a vital part of the organisational ecosystem. I, personally, have worked for years with an organisation at lower salary as compared with some of my counterparts, because I felt secure in the value and recognition I was given. I remember an instance when, while working in the same organisation, I saw changes in the workings of the management, where they were not respecting my individuality and I did not feel truly involved, I started exploring other options elsewhere. There were many brands who were willing to offer me substantially more remuneration. If a business values an employee, the latter will willingly continue being a part of that business for years, never thinking of moving out.

E for Exciting work and challenge—Although it is said that most people are comfortable with an easy life, the dichotomy persists that work which is not challenging, which does not make one feel excited about doing it can't hold a person to it for a long time. People who play computer games will be familiar with the feeling of ecstasy they experience every time they cross one hurdle and make it to the next, even more complex level. They become addicted to the game as this sense of challenge gives them a real kick. To quote an example here, when my son joined a mass media course of study in college, initially, he didn't find it exciting. Time and again, he would tell me that he wanted to switch to another college. Within a year, he discovered that his interest lay in being accountable for conducting college events and bringing innovation to them through his efforts. He started working hard day in and day out to harness his talents and deliver on what he enjoyed doing most, and the way he blossomed as an individual came as a lovely surprise to many of us.

S for Supportive management—People can do a job well only if they have the right support whenever they are stuck in a difficult or sticky situation. If the management or boss is there to back them, employees will feel comfortable and will give their best to ensure the tasks in hand are completed successfully within the stipulated timelines. However, this does not mean that employees can be lax about discipline when it comes to systems, processes and other required compliance parameters. They must be dealt with firmly when they do not adhere to standard operating processes. Support only means genuine concern for people working with you and creating a path for them to grow. It involves helping them use their strengths for the benefit of business and working on their weaknesses to help them become better professionals, better people.

The most important part of leadership is creating a competent team of people under you who can help you drive a vision. When a leader assists people to climb to the next rung of the ladder, the leader will automatically move to a higher level too, also ensuring that the organisation too reaches its goals by creating competent people who can be a part of organisational goal realisation. It may sound idealistic, but my years of experience have taught me that it is precisely such people who propel a business forward on the path of long-term success.

Nevertheless, one must remember that people will always emulate the leadership. If the leader is committed, the team will also display high standards of commitment. However, if leaders keep asking subordinates to do things and do not bring the same level of involvement to the table themselves, the team will also slacken in its commitment to the job.

P for Pay and benefits—Money is a necessity of life and materialism a necessary evil. Human aspirations are built around the luxuries of life which only money can buy. High salaries are part of aspirational values and give people a feel of success. Hence, if the pay is competitive and there are also fringe benefits offered, people stick around longer in an organisation. Peer pressure from friends and family earning more is one reason for jumping jobs. An organisation must build a business model keeping this important fact in mind because the right people are the ones who steer an organisation to success, but they come at a price.

Many organisations win the support of the employee's family by incorporating employee-centric schemes that seek to provide benefits for the employee and his family members. For example, firms that offer fringe benefits, such as medical benefits, not only to the employee but also to his family members would definitely be sought-after employers.

E for Engagement—People like to be given importance and be involved in what is happening for only then do they feel they are a vital part of a venture. An organisation is ideally on a mission to create good products and services, creating great client experience, thereby attracting high revenues. Employees are a part of this mission to help a brand achieve all its objectives. If they do not feel involved, they will not give their best. The style of engagement that an organisation should follow is of two types. Firstly, engaging the employee in daily tasks through discussion, ideation, appreciation, and involvement on the way forward. Such employees are wholly oriented to the tasks set out for them. People who are not engaged and reviewed end up whiling away time. The second kind of engagement involves employees' families. I grew up in a defence background and was privy to how the officials' families were made to interact through workshops, ladies' club meets, and family functions, all of which helped them to become the solid foundation that allows defence personnel to live for long periods of time under stringent conditions away from their families. Similarly, I recall a colleague whose wife worked in a prestigious city school and the family used to really look forward to the annual Diwali bash hosted by the celebrity promoter where she invited all family members of the teaching staff.

Engagement is a critical factor that determines people's sustained desire to be a part of an organisation.

C for Conducive culture: An organisation's culture is really what defines its success. If the environment gives people the space to be creative and, at the same time, fosters productivity, people stick around for a longer time. There has to be respect accorded to all employees. A company where people feel the power of their seat and do not respect subordinates can never be conducive to lasting growth. Think of an instance when you joined an organisation where people encouraged you, treated you with dignity, and set expectations with you for delivery. You would have happily done what is required. But where tempers fly and bosses and/or management cross the line of respect, there is discontent and attrition.

T for Trust and clear communication—This is the base of the edifice of success in any organisation. If there is lack of trust within people working together and lack of proper communication, misunderstandings crop up. Most instances of individual conflict occur when people do not communicate with one other openly. A gap in communication causes people to start suspecting that the other party is plotting against them. It is critical that managers communicate with employees daily, and in case of misunderstandings or disagreements, they must always speak directly in putting forth their point to the employee. They must also always keep an open mind as the subordinate or peer could have a point which merits attention. This is the best way to resolve any people issues that arise.

People need to feel emotionally involved with their work and they need to feel a connection with the organisation they work for. This would require trying to understand their needs and orienting and aligning them with organisational needs. If a company is able to build this kind of connection with the employees, productivity is significantly enhanced.

Organisations which understand the simple fabric of building the right HR policies, keeping the external environment and market standards in mind, end up building the right teams who work concertedly in a conducive environment towards achieving organisational goals.

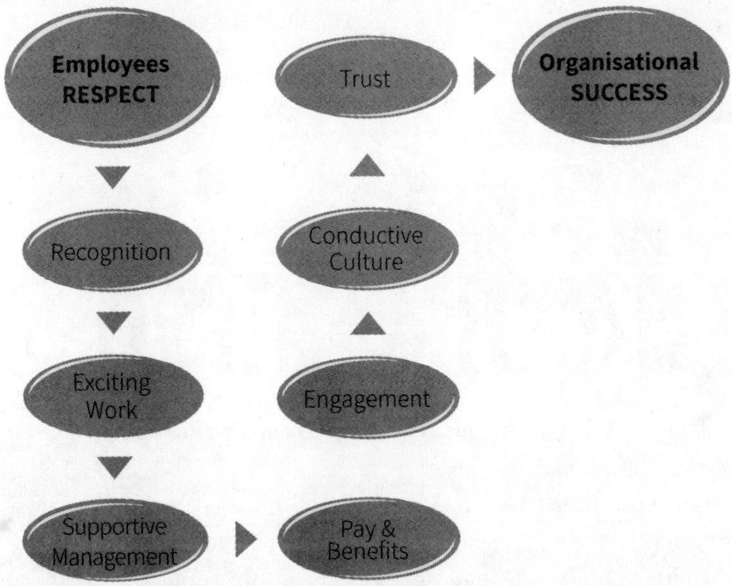

HR: RESPECT Drives Organisational Success

9

Standard Operating Procedures

SOPs: The Guru Mantra to Scaling Business

When you speak to a start-up entrepreneur, one of the most frequently posed questions is—How do I scale up my business? If I hire people, will they be able to live up to my vision? Many entrepreneurs end up being all over the place, unable to strategise and focus on the most important quadrant of their work. The only solution is to set down strong processes and ensure adherence to the same. An organisation can function effectively only when there are clearly defined processes called Standard Operating Procedures.

When I was a branch manager with a leading multi-level marketing company, we were taught during the 'Train the Trainer' programme about the importance of carrying along a folder for a sales pitch. Initially, being a successful sales person, and having always been impromptu in my sales pitch, I wondered how I could speak with a folder in hand, reading from a sheet of paper, and how I would teach the team to follow the same practice. However, thinking rationally, I realised there was merit in the method, as it made the sales process easy to replicate. It was quite a task to get independent sales consultants to start believing in this seemingly simple process—carrying a folder and using it to make the entire pitch.

I decided to hold a meeting for all the managers and leaders in the system and introduce the concept of the folder. I played the Chinese Whispers game to show them how in the method being used so far to train their teams, information passed around got diluted and altogether changed when passed on verbally, whereas how a written paper in a folder would make the entire process simpler and more accurate. They believed in the conceptual merit of it, yet they voiced their concern about how someone could emulate this process of reading out a sales pitch. So I set up an experiment. I told them I needed a volunteer from amongst them who could spare 10 days to participate in 7 to 8 meetings with me. We needed to have fixed daily appointments for me to show how this folder could change their lives. A lady who was gregarious by nature, who was among the 9 to 12 per cent level on the business ladder defined by the company, earning approximately ₹5000 to ₹6000, agreed to participate. Thus began the experiment. She and I lived in two far-flung corners of the city, but every morning,

I would pick her up from her place in my car and go visit the friends whom she had fixed appointments with. We were able to cover about 6 meetings on an average, and every day, I made the pitch using the folder. What we saw was that each time, either we ended up selling products, or the customer signed up as a sales consultant. After some days, the lady too started using the folder to make the pitch exactly as it was mentioned in the folder. At the end of 10 days, she had risen in rank to join the 18 per cent senior manager bracket, just slightly short of being a director, and her earnings had grown over three times what they had been, which was a great boost to both her belief as well as the conviction of all the leaders and managers in the system and its processes. Thereafter, I was able to impart training and get all the leaders to use the folder. Soon, the positive impact was widely felt and the blue folder became the trademark of the business. The success rate of the folder method was highest in my branch as more and more people began to believe in the power of following a written process.

A written process clearly defines what needs to be done, providing clarity on how, when and who needs to do the task.

What are Standard Operating Procedures?

Standard Operating Procedures (better known as SOPs) are the documented processes that a company sets in place to ensure services/products are delivered consistently. When a company is growing, all decisions are often taken by the owner but as the company attains a certain size, this form of decision making can limit its capacity to grow further since the owner cannot possibly do justice to all the work entailed in running the organisation as it expands. Furthermore, the founder may not be proficient in all aspects of the business and may need to delegate to specialists. To ensure that the work is carried out properly without error, it is best to have SOPs to ensure that people earmarked to perform certain tasks know why, when and how they need to be done. Additional management and documented SOPs are required to allow the company to continue growing, to establish a succession plan and to train the expanding employee base.

SOPs provide a clear path that the employee needs to follow, whereby chances of making mistakes are minimised. It is not that employees will not make mistakes at all, but the margin of error will drastically go down. It is humanly impossible for entrepreneurs to do everything on their own, and if they try to do so, they will never create leadership in the organisation. For any company to grow, there have to be key people who follow due processes as per the pre-set SOPs and ascertain delivery of the same.

SOPs should be made taking into consideration the specialisations of the team members driving a particular function in discussion with the entrepreneur and the management team, if any. The subsequent document created called the standard operating folder should be kept in a common folder accessible to all employees who must be given uniform training and explanations before they begin work.

While making an SOP, the following aspects need to be clearly addressed:

1. Why the SOP is being made, what are its objectives, and what it wants to ensure.

2. When and how often the SOP should be followed. Certain SOPs may need to be adhered to daily, some weekly, others on a monthly or quarterly review basis. For example, every month, legal trade licenses could require a review SOP.

3. Who is going to follow the SOP and who is accountable for following it. There must be specific names and designations assigned under the 'who' behind the SOP.

4. By whom will the review of the SOP be done on a regular basis to ensure adherence to the same.

By and large, the SOPs followed by any organisation are outlined below:

1. **Strategic SOPs:** These are broad-based SOPs that describe the strategic processes that senior management must follow to attain both long-term and short-term goals of an organisation. However, not everything needs to rest with the entrepreneur/business head for that would defeat the purpose of having individual heads for every functional area. More minds working together have the ability to create much better results, and strategic SOPs must come to bear on how decision making takes place in an organisation.

   In any venture, the person at the top needs to work in tandem with a team, delegating when necessary, for the business to prosper.

   Here's a story that illustrates this point.

   There was an entrepreneur who had scaled up his business to a certain level with the help of a team he worked with. After a couple of years, there came a point when he wanted to drive every decision within the organisation. Right from what sales schemes needed to be implemented, how the manpower available had to be placed, what the marketing plans should be, what structure should be followed in terms of hiring—he wanted to be the one to take every decision in running the business. But in the process of trying to bring everything under his direct control, he didn't realise that productivity and motivation levels began dropping. Suddenly, the people who were working for him found themselves incapable of taking any decision whereas accountability for the work still rested on their shoulders. In such a scenario, the hitherto growing organisation soon began to collapse. The team was unable to deliver as deadlines were missed. Reviews of work faltered because every time a review was held, the team had the same explanation, that this was what the entrepreneur had said needed to be done, or that it was lying at his desk for approval. As a result, despite having enjoyed a long stint of growth, the organisation now began to de-grow, as team heads were unable to take any decision nor could they contribute to the think tank process that is so essential for expansion in any sphere of development.

Hence, it is critical that entrepreneurs develop a strategic, long-term goal and delegate work ideation and review to functional heads, as defined in the company's SOPs.

2. **Billing procedures and product/service delivery:** Revenue is what primarily drives an organisation. Therefore, it is of paramount importance that this SOP should be very clearly defined in order to ensure correct revenue billing, to plug in any gaps and leakages that may creep in. Most businesses must create a robust online system and the reigns of control must lie in the hands of the finance head, or the entrepreneur.

   I have seen many cases where a firm builds a model for air conditioning services delivered at the doorstep and the employees start obtaining repeat orders for business networking at a personal level. This results in revenue loss, as they provide discounted services, falsely stating that the company charges higher rates. To avoid such losses, the billing process can instead be digitalised.

   Let me narrate my own experience. Some years ago, an AC company service engineer came to my house and after checking the machine, he told me that the gas needed replacing as well, and there was a problem in the fan. He quoted a certain amount apparently charged by the company and said he would do the job in personal capacity at one-third the charge. In a way, he was cheating the company he was employed with, causing revenue leakage. A couple of years later, I called a technician of the same company to repair my microwave oven. This service staff was using an automated system, so he didn't offhand have details about pricing, etc. The minute he keyed into his system the names of the parts to be replaced, the billing details were forwarded via SMS to my mobile number. I paid him and he too received all details regarding the payment on the app.

Additionally, the billing system should be such that the option to edit bills after a bill is generated must not rest with the cashier. And if the cashier does make a change in the bill, intimation regarding such action must automatically be sent to a senior in charge of revenues, or to the entrepreneur, to prevent the cashier from defrauding the system. I have seen such instances even in big organisations. The billing system must be designed in a robust manner so as to do away with any chance of revenue leakages.

Most importantly, the finance department in an organisation must have a strong audit system in place, which may even involve taking feedback from the consumer, or the sending of a message to the consumer after billing, stating, "Thank you for your payment of ₹xxx." Manual hand bills need to be replaced by soft copies of the bill sent to the customer via email.

3. **Inventory management system:** Inventory blocks working capital, and so there are SOPs that need to be framed in lieu of that. There needs to be a pre-defined process to maintain and keep track of any consumables. These must be digitalised, so that review managers have knowledge of where and what the batch of inventory is. The FIFO (First In First Out) mechanism must be followed in dispensing the stock to avoid losses on account of stock expiring.

   To avoid blocking working capital in excess inventory, the business can follow the principle of Economic Order

Quantity (EOQ). This is the order quantity that minimises total holding and ordering costs for the year. Even if all assumptions made while ordering don't pan out exactly, the EOQ gives a good indication of whether or not the ordered quantities are reasonable.

Simple procedures, such as barcoding, must be implemented. These processes are quite affordable and ensure full control of inventory management. When businesses expand without working on creating such processes and setting up weekly reviews, it affects the bottom line as the resultant leakages negatively impact profitability.

4. **Sales process SOPs:** There must be well-tailored SOPs for every part of the sales process, defining in detail how the entire sales flow will take place. Sales, as we discussed earlier, is a science, which is why it is important to have clearly outlined steps and broad guideline scripts to facilitate duplication of the process so it can easily be followed by everyone. Target setting and review SOPs are a mandatory component of the sales process. Moreover, keeping in mind the business vision, customer-centric processes need to be incorporated. I remember reading about how the Big Basket team had clearly defined SOPs laying emphasis on even the smallest of customer service gestures which would go a long way in building the brand in the eyes of the customer. In the sales delivery process, the locked baskets had to opened in front of the customer and the little piece of plastic used in tying up the basket must be picked up by the delivery person. This is their way of making sure the customer does not later on find their house littered, and does not injure their foot by stepping on the plastic piece.

5. **Marketing process SOPs:** The marketing SOP may need to outline how to conduct the strategy meeting to create the

marketing plan, followed by how to review the marketing plan. It needs to factor in the process for POP (Point of Purchase material) and marketing communication to be designed and placed. Other things that need considering include how the audit process would take place to see if operationally marketing POP and merchandise placement has happened, and how to go about seeking necessary approval for art work.

The most important SOP that a brand needs to have in place is one that will review the ROI (returns on investment) of marketing activity, which would help understand the strengths and weaknesses of the campaign. That way, the team can work towards improving future campaigns based on the ROI evaluation and the brand awareness and goodwill generated. Most people are of the opinion that measuring brand campaigns is a long-term exercise, but small surveys and sales impact help in understanding the effectiveness of a campaign. The objective of marketing is creating customers, and if that is not achieved in the stipulated period set by the branding team, then however brilliant their campaign seems, it needs to be reworked. SOPs that analyse this aspect keep the organisation on track.

6. **Brand tarnish SOPs:** Always define the SOPs which could dilute your brand and result in financial or brand value loss. These must be non-negotiable in terms of adherence. The team must have a policy of blacklisting for not adhering to them. Constant breach of these terms should be met with severe penalisation.

7. **Statutory SOPs:** Every business needs to be vigilant with regard to government regulations, laws and statutory compliances. Hence, it must clearly define who is accountable for ensuring adherence to the same and also for keeping abreast of new regulations. There could be certain licenses

required to begin the business, GST registration and timely payments to be made, ESIC and labour law adherence, sales tax, etc. The why, when, who, and whom of all such aspects must be thoroughly delineated to avoid any default in following statutory procedures and licensing in an organisation.

8. **Legal SOPs:** Legal SOPs to handle irate customers, employees, emergencies cropping up in business must be laid down with clarity. There has to be a designated person who can address these as well as a procedure in place to get across to concerned person along with escalation points, if any.

   Drills need to be conducted within the organisation, akin to fire drills, for employees to understand threadbare all SOPs laid down by the authorities. There must be mocks and refresher training programmes held in customer service training to educate staff on emergency SOPs, irate customer handling SOP, and so on.

9. **Administrative SOPs:** There have to be SOPs in place for phone and Internet usage, petty cash, travel, and other administrative tasks, so that everyone is aware and able to maintain transparency in the system.

10. **Human resources:** People drive an organisation. There must be clear dos and don'ts laid down as per the company's HR policy, covering aspects such as the attendance process, payslip, leave policy, etc., so that all employees know whom to approach in case of need.

11. **IT SOPs:** Information technology (IT) plays a critical role in today's times, mandating the usage of IT resources within the office, confidentiality of data, and diligent adherence to processes of CRM systems. A start-up must invest in a CRM system; there are many free platforms available as well. Alternatively, a CRM system can be customised as per need, if what is available does not match what one is looking for.

12. **Customer service SOPs:** This is a critical SOP which is part of every step of customer engagement, right from fixing an appointment to explaining the product, to closing the sale and implementing after-sales service, for it is customer service experiences that create brands.

13. **Call Centre SOPs:** If the company has a call centre service, then SOPs for rostering, the scripts to be followed while answering, review, quality feedback, and quality improvement, along with target setting must be incorporated.

14. **Training SOPs:** The right kind of training and assessment procedures will align your people to the brand vision and help you achieve the brand mission. There must be a regular process of refresher training sessions conducted to make sure the task force do not lose their edge.

    It is vital to note that SOPs are not made to be reflected only on paper. The primary objective of an SOP is to drive efficiencies within an organisation, and that is possible only by creating a robust system to audit the implementation of these SOPs. Only then will the organisation as a unit be efficient and productive.

10

Customer Intelligence, Engagement Model Analytics, and AI

The more you know about your customer, the better you can serve him. In the present competitive age, information is king. Brands that are able to leverage customer information and use it to their advantage can substantially expand their business. Google, when it first started functioning as a search engine, was a brand that allowed people to manage their information online. But in the process of doing so, it began building links, interlinks, and information about people to the extent that soon they realised there was a great opportunity to be tapped here. They could monetize the advantage they had by getting people to use keywords and by way of digital advertising. Today, by adding multiple platforms, such as Gmail, YouTube, Google Plus, and so on, Google has created an excellent business platform for itself, making it one of the biggest companies in terms of business turnover.

Customer loyalty is based on the experiential journey of the customer with the business. However, even a great customer service team can fail, because in a dynamic market, one needs to keep evolving and in such a state, the customer looks for the best value experience. Hence, it becomes essential for a business to keep mining data so as to understand the changes in trends as well as predict future trends, which would allow them to retain a grip on the pulse of changing customer needs. This is possible only by using effective customer data mining tools and combining it with machine learning to be able to predict consumer behaviour and use it to drive business productivity. Businesses can successfully use customer intelligence to engage them and create opportunities to make the customer experience delightful as well as to substantially increase the ticket size per customer. If handled properly, it can create a lifelong customer.

But how does customer intelligence work? The customer intelligence model looks at multiple parameters of customer data, ranging from demographic information and time spent on online marketing, to purchase patterns, feedback given, and social details about them obtained from their engagement on public media. The model then leverages all this information to create algorithms to predict behaviour by analysing the behaviour of past customers following the same trends.

Customer intelligence analysis is based on data mining. Data mining is the process of finding anomalies, patterns, and correlations within large data sets to predict outcomes. Using a broad range of techniques, one can use this information to increase revenue, cut costs, improve customer relationships, reduce risk, etc.

Data mining works on two key factors, the first being Artificial Intelligence (AI, a software that displays human-like intelligence) and the second being machine learning (which comprises algorithms that learn from data to predict behaviour). Advance in technology in the field of AI and business analytics have managed to do away with tedious, manual practices. The more complex the data sets collected, the better the chance to uncover relevant insights. In today's times, all kinds of businesses, right from retail to banks to manufacturers to e-commerce, are using data mining and analytics to create a competitive edge by correlating relationships between marketing strategies, such as pricing/promotion, marketing communication, government policies, risk, competition, and by understanding how businesses are getting impacted by them.

It is an extremely powerful tool that can be used to tap leakage and wastage in the productivity cycle as also to control fresh marketing costs. Nevertheless, this is easier said than done. Organisations need to be fully aware of why they plan to gather the data, and what is the outcome they intend to achieve from that data which will benefit them. If there is clarity of purpose, the IT team along with the concerned departments can get people to contribute to worthwhile usage of data to draw inferences and help the organisation be productive.

When a business starts understanding what products customers are interested in or what they have bought, they can create relevant marketing communication around the same. The customer intelligence tool also has the ability to give feedback on which platform—social media/SMS/email—the customer logs into and at approximately what time, so that the communication can, furthermore, be customised to that medium and that preferred time, offering a better chance of engaging with the customer. Once customer intelligence is ready, it can be clubbed with customer engagement tools and AI to increase productivity.

Many times, when people draw up the end purpose of using data, they realise that the data they have is either of low quality or missing too many points to make meaningful comprehension. I remember how in one of the organisations I worked with, we had lots of data at our disposal but when we attempted to study its lineage and lifespan, we struggled to get 100 per cent accuracy. There were human errors in capturing certain data points, including contact numbers/email ids, as the CRM system migration, years ago, had not been effected seamlessly. Or, the billing system hadn't properly captured customer lineage and was merely a receipt/invoice system, whereby it was difficult to use data that was a couple of years old to comprehend information cohesively, which then became a learning point to enable more accurate gathering of data in the future. It is also imperative that an organisation collaborates with specialised companies to use the data effectively. I recall that in the same organisation, we experienced multiple phases in building productivity, thanks to initially using a business intelligence tool which was unable to yield productivity for a long period of time, even though we were able to build some data points by integrating the CRM systems with the tool. However, collaboration with customer intelligence vendors enabled us to build up the data to a level that allowed for more comprehensive understanding, paving the way to better productivity.

Just as Research and Development (R&D) has become an important aspect of business growth, with several firms deploying big teams to work on their product, its development and innovation, so too has customer data, his engagement with your brand and the enhancement of his life cycle with your product become the key driver to success. Hence, it is imperative that the customer data be studied by a technical team which is able to understand the patterns therein of buying, dropping out, competitive change, and repeat purchase, which can then come up with a strategy to deliver more and remarket to your customer so as to make him a lifetime client for the firm's product and services.

The main ways in which a business can benefit from customer intelligence and engagement are described below. It is desirable that when the teams work towards these objectives, they define how they will realise the end purpose and what the important timelines and patterns they would follow to arrive there.

1. **Real-time feedback and customer insights:** One gets real-time feedback by understanding the positive/negative words/text used in feedback forms as well as on social media and using that understanding to work on improving customer experience. If such feedback reaches the concerned authorities in real time, the latter can address the problem and help build customer delight. Instant action taken to facilitate customer satisfaction can build loyalty towards the brand, as it makes the customer feel important and perceive that the brand genuinely cares for them.

2. **Prompt and better service:** Use of customer intelligence coupled with AI can enhance customer experience. For example, if you call a helpline for service brands, such as Go Daddy or a travel portal, you are first directed to a chat window where you get help with basic queries, basic solutions, which then connects you to the human customer service team in case of any further complex issues. This not only allows them to address more customer queries, but also saves on time and money spent on the business, while improving customer experience. Similarly, there are virtual assistants who can offer service beyond regular working hours and help a customer shop or book appointments with ease.

3. **Building loyalty:** Customer intelligence helps the organisation gather data on the needs and activities of the customer, based on which relevant targeting can be done to enhance customer experience, and, as a result, improve loyalty. Based on similar profiling of customer data, one can predict patterns and pitch a relevant product/service, thereby building brand loyalty.

4. **Keeping the business on the growth trajectory:** In a dynamic business world where internal/external changes are constantly happening, quick decision making based on customer intelligence and predictive analysis when these issues crop up keeps the business on track.

5. **Customer engagement leading to new insights:** With a secure online medium available, one can test and understand customer behaviour and reach out to the customer in order to comprehend customer insights that help build marketing strategies. Such customer engagement also reduces costs and increases productivity and growth. Many brands have used customer surveys to successfully launch new products and services.

6. **Competitive advantage:** Customer intelligence aids in differentiating customer experiences and creating a value proposition, thereby allowing the business to develop a competitive edge.

7. **Upselling and cross-selling:** Understanding past trends with similar audiences across various parameters, one can evaluate opportunities to upsell and cross-sell, thereby increasing ticket size.

8. **Increasing the life cycle of a customer:** Understanding the trends seen in case of loyal customers and applying this intelligence to analyse other, like-minded audiences can enhance customer experience and keep him engaged, increasing the overall customer life cycle.

9. **Increasing referral:** Customer intelligence and engagement through innovative marketing to loyal customers can help a brand substantially reduce the cost of marketing by creating walking-talking brand ambassadors who will bring referral customers into the business.

10. **Marketing plan and efficiency levels:** Customer intelligence delves into business campaigns carried out across various online platforms, studies their efficiency levels, correlates with what the competition is doing, and then chalks out an efficient marketing plan.

The Top 100 companies of 2018 listing saw Amazon topping the list. The ground work for this achievement was based on the ability to understand individual consumer habits by focusing on analytics and data intelligence along with enhancing profitability. Joseph Sirosh, CTO of Compass, joined Amazon in 2004, and was instrumental in reducing both fraud and bad debt and the number of customers who didn't get their goods and suppliers who didn't get their money, by working aggressively on creating a team which conceived and built the Amazon machine learning system. By the time he left Amazon in 2013, Sirosh's group had grown from 35 to more than 1000 people who used machine learning to make Amazon more operationally efficient and effective. Over the same time period, the company saw a ten-fold increase in revenue.

There are a plethora of customer intelligence tools and customer engagement programmes based on AI which can be evaluated based on their suitability to one's business, taking into account efficiency levels as well as costs involved.

Businesses which understand the importance of analysing customer behaviour via multiple parameters and engaging with them productively are able to service customers better at lower costs and, in the process, also boost productivity and growth. However, the importance of human empathy and emotional intelligence can't be done away with. Organisations can build on customer experience by effectively using customer intelligence and AI and having a proactive strategy team and customer service team engaging with the customer.

It is imperative to have proper reports generated using these two tools, and the impact of actions taken must be reviewed. The action required must be set with defined timelines so that the hard work of mining and predicting customer data brings about the desired end result of productivity enhancement.

DESSERTS

11

Franchise versus Own Business

In my association with many start-up businesses, I have always come across one common dilemma they all face. Funding is tight and they want to expand, but they don't really know which is the best way to grow—opening a franchise or setting up their own business module.

There are many brands which have built great business models based on franchising. Franchising provides faster growth possibilities as the business gets money to expand because it is based on investment from franchisees.

Lakme Salons and Jawed Habib are two such models that have seen huge business growth based on the franchise module. Jawed Habib, coming from a family of hairdressers, decided to build an organised unisex salon early in his life, after undergoing training in London. As he opted for the franchise route, categorising his ventures under three different models—the Jawed Habib Hair and Beauty Studio Private Limited, Jawed Habib's Hair Xpreso Private Ltd, and Habib's Hair and Beauty Studio Private Limited—he was able to build a big business empire that runs in over 100 cities, with 800 plus salons. Armed with astute business acumen, he worked on creating an acceptable model and was able to build the brand up to that scale. However, as this business is skill-based and dependent on individual performance, unlike the food business which can be mechanised, he faced many challenges, which ultimately resulted in dilution of the brand image in many places. Well aware of this flipside, he put in effort to create a good training academy to ensure that the skill set and expertise level would be maintained. But manning and controlling a business of this size, which required the brand experience to be delivered consistently as per set standards, became difficult.

So, he decided to classify affordable salons at ₹99 for a haircut at the Xpreso outlets. The one-time franchisee fee along with recurring royalty helped retain the EBITDA (Earnings Before Interest, Depreciation, and Amortization) and PAT (Profit After Tax) on the positive side although they could have been better if the business had expanded with more digitalised control.

Similarly, Lakme Salons was able to come up with an extension of their personal care brand based on a franchise model. Today, the brand boasts of 280 plus salons spread over the country, of which 85 per cent are franchisees.

If you are evaluating your options, trying to decide between expanding your business on your own versus franchising it out, you need to understand the pros and cons of both, keeping your business in mind. Some businesses which are based on mechanised systems and do not need advanced human skill sets, can easily be replicated and followed by most people. But some others, such as those involving surgical procedures, hair cutting/dressing, manual artefacts, etc., involve varying levels of specialisation which necessitate intensive training. Furthermore, if the replication is difficult, it may adversely impact your brand, watering down the brand.

When I joined a specialised clinical business, I observed that the brand was compromised in many markets as regulatory mechanisms were not in place. Besides, the specialised business segments, where patient results were the barometer of business success, were getting a raw deal, as some franchisees were using short-term routes to earn money by not giving holistic or customised treatments wherever they earned heavy margins. This naturally led to customers not being able to avail of the best results. The first couple of years of my joining the firm were largely devoted to buying over such miscreant franchisees.

One needs to tread very carefully on the franchise route by first putting the right systems, monitoring, and audit tools, training processes, etc., in place to guarantee that brand experience and results don't get diluted.

It is important to understand what a franchise is. A franchise is a legal and commercial agreement between the owner of a trademark/brand name/service brand (known as franchisor) and an individual/organisation (known as franchisee) to use the trademark/brand name/service brand as an identification of business. A franchisee has to run the business module based on the guidelines/procedures set down by the franchisor.

Let us look at the pros and cons of franchising a business.

Pros:

1. **Easy and fast expansion of business as financial investment is not a burden on the parent company:** In franchising models, financial investment on rent/interiors/working capital/manpower, etc., is borne by the franchisee. Hence, the business does not feel the strain of expansion, and if a partner is available and suits the business requirements, it can enjoy quick expansion.

2. Cash inflow begins as soon as the franchise is signed on, as there could be a franchisee fee and royalty that the franchisee has to pay.

3. Marketing burden can be shared by the franchisee.

4. Brand reach and growth is fast in this model as the franchisee partner also shoulders local responsibility for brand creation and market growth.

Cons:

1. To set up the franchise, one needs to finance the start-up cost to get the franchisee going in the business.

2. To set up a franchise-based business model, brand awareness needs to be created by spending on marketing, training and manpower.

3. There could be a dilution of the brand if proper regulatory processes are not in place. Also, laxity in not revamping outlets, if that is not enshrined in a written agreement, can diminish the brand.

4. As there are certain terms of agreement involved in franchising, making any changes to the business module may require detailed thought and agreement between the two parties.

5. In case the franchise fails, the business owner may need to buy back the franchise.

Before you choose between expansion via growing your own business or taking up the franchise module, you must understand the market potential thoroughly and the way your business would need to be modelled if it had to expand in the market.

Business expansion is possible if you understand how you can get the market ready for your product. Let me share the story of Café Coffee Day. The founder, V G Siddhartha, was born to a plantation owner. Young Siddhartha began his career trading in the stock market. Soon he began investing in coffee plantations adding to his father's existing plantations, thereby becoming the owner of huge coffee plantations that were four times those run by his father.

A meeting with a director of Tchibo, a German coffee brand, gave him the idea for a retail business in coffee shops. But he was discouraged by professionals who worked with him who asked him why anyone would buy coffee worth ₹15 from them when it was available at ₹5 round the corner. A chance visit to a beer shop in Singapore that offered free internet access made him think of creating something similar, replacing beer with coffee. His vision saw the birth of Café Coffee Day, a brand that today boasts of over 1500 outlets spread across the country. He could create a splendid business model only because he clearly understood the business potential at hand as well as his own strengths, considering he was a coffee plantation owner's son.

Café Coffee Day does not franchise its business, but it has created a business module wherein it only collaborates with people who own retail space as per the specifications of Café Coffee Day. The running of these collaborative spaces is also managed by Café Coffee Day, the parent company. This approach has proved to be very beneficial for them.

Hence, the decision to run your own business versus a franchising module has to be based on careful evaluation of your ability to scale up the business based on self-financing and easy funding options, ability to replicate the business module, your core strengths, and your long-term vision for the brand.

Franchising offers scope for faster scaling up of a business, wherein the organisation can depend on the franchisee partner to bring in money and can have collaborative business models alongside.

Some franchise modules prevalent in practice are outlined below:

1. **FIFO (Franchisee-Invested Franchisee-Operated):** In this model, the franchisee not only invests in the franchise but is also responsible for operating it. This is the most popular model from the franchisee perspective as people like to be involved in running a business they have invested in. However, for a first-time franchisee, the risk element is higher in this model, as the skill and prowess ploughed into running the business is his own, even though the parent company provided training, mentoring, and marketing support.

2. **FICO (Franchisee-Invested, Company-Operated):** In this model, the organisation grows based on the financial prowess of the franchisee partner. But at the same time, it safeguards the brand as the franchise is run by the parent company.

Over time, it has been found that most brands prefer this mode of operation because it entails minimum risk to the franchisee who receives returns on investment, and at the same time, the parent company stakes are high so as to maintain profitability. Moreover, the company is able to expand its business while ensuring brand quality is maintained as responsibility for operating the franchised outlet lies with it. What's more, the entire top line of the franchise is a part of the company top line.

3. **CICO (Company-Invested Company-Operated):** This is the preferred choice if the company is able to fund its growth by raising capital. However, expansion plans can be slower if a company follows only the CICO model.

   Thus, a brand needs to examine its long-term and short-term business plan and understand the organisational goals that will help it in the long run by building both profitability and growth. Based on these considerations, it can devise a suitable franchise strategy.

12

Cash Flow Management and Funding

Most businesses are born as a brilliant idea, but only 15 to 20 per cent are able to sail through on the entrepreneurial journey. This owes largely to cash deficits in keeping the business running. In such a case, it is of utmost importance to not only have an effective business plan but also have strong strategic reviews to understand gaps in profits based on the business plan. A business may require infusion of money from time to time, but it cannot be successful by merely constantly working through by bringing in new debt.

Effective management and strategy are essential ingredients for business success. No doubt, every entrepreneur strives to make money. But business management is all about reviewing the financial health of the unit, and planning and executing strategy accordingly. Even as a business works on giving the best product and service to its customers, it must run internal operations, especially during the growth stage, as frugally as possible. Walmart's business model succeeded not only because of the entrepreneurial passion and management style of Sam Walton but also because of the frugal business operations he ran, particularly in the initial years when cash was really tight.

Markets and customer needs are constantly evolving. Hence, keeping business strategy tied in with cash flow management is the key to long-term business success.

The Jet Airways debacle occurring after more than two decades of successful operation is a classic case of how poor cash flow management coupled with lack of strategic changes required in an evolving market can kill a business.

Jet Airways began operations as the leader in the private aviation sector in India, building an image of high-end customer service with aggressive loyalty schemes catering to the corporate flyer. But a few years down the line, it ran into problems. Firstly, it failed to keep a check on mounting costs and secondly, it underestimated the power wielded by low-cost airlines in a price-sensitive, evolving Indian market. It is only natural that mistakes will be made in any business. But if the mistakes are not understood and if strategic, timely redressals are not effected, the business will suffer in the long run. Jet Airways' error lay in not managing cash flow properly and repeatedly increasing debt. Trouble began brewing when it decided to invest heavily in buying Sahara Airlines at 500 million dollars, a price that many analysts felt was too high. Furthermore, Jet Airways kept borrowing to tide over cash flow crunches, even when the bulk of their expenses were on the higher side in comparison with Indian aviation industry standards. For instance, their manpower costs were 30 per cent higher than the competition. They continued to provide free meals, even though their tickets were priced at more or less the same level as that charged by budget carriers. Also, they were unable to build any inflight revenue, as a result of which the business model began losing viability while fuel costs kept shooting up. The brand failed to strategically revamp the business model and continued borrowing to keep itself afloat. The repercussions were such that things came to a stage where the airline had no cash reserves left, so much so that they could neither pay the employees nor operate flights. Soon, they declared bankruptcy, as none of the investors wanted to invest further in a mismanaged organisation, and lender pressure to recover dues caused the airline to shut shop.

Cash flow is the lifeline that keeps an organisation afloat. That is why proper planning and assessment of an organisation's cash flow, while keeping in mind fluctuations that may occur in revenue earning, is an absolute must. Even though top line growth needs to be the main focus, the bottom line in a company must be protected by working on keeping costs under control.

High-debt units face a challenge, because even though profits may be registered, high borrowing costs can strain cash flow and make it difficult to meet ends. Expansion of a business at the cost of substantially compromising the return of capital may not be viable in the long run.

A business model must be built on scalability and profitability. Obviously, there is a break-even period in any business, and cash flow must be planned in such a manner as to ensure there is surplus cash to tide over the calculated break-even cycle at least two times. A bootstrapped business may face a challenge in such a scenario, which is why it becomes critical that planning and execution of the business plan in start-ups must continually work on at least building operating profitability to maintain reasonable cash flow in case of adverse circumstances. Start-ups must exercise extremely nifty cash control management, coaching, and mentoring team members on the importance of keeping operating costs tight without compromising on the quality of products and customer service, as this will be the first step towards building revenue and, thereby, better cash flow. The entrepreneur must lead by example. Manpower costs, however, should not be compromised and should remain competitive as the right manpower is key to building and growing the business.

Cash flow is basically the process of tracking, analytically assessing, and optimising net cash inflow after subtracting cash expenses.

Let's understand how cash flow management helps an entrepreneur:

1. Cash flow lets a business understand future needs to keep the business on track as well as strategically plan to grow the business accordingly.

2. Cash flow planning allows the team to develop sales targets and to understand sales gap planning to avoid crisis.

3. It aids the prioritising and optimising of cash expenses.
4. It helps plan timely statutory payment and debt repayment.
5. It allows the management to present a correct picture to investors of the cash flow health of the organisation.
6. Cash flow management helps invest excess cash reserves to improve financial returns.
7. Cash flow management facilitates timely recovery of receivables.
8. It helps to manage creditors better by optimising cash rotation effectively.
9. It provides strategic input to the management team for them to understand changes in patterns and business trends and thereby proactively work towards business goal realisation.

Cash flow management is the tool that aids in planning financial management of any organisation. There must be clarity about how to fill the gaps and strategically plan business delivery if there is a consistent deficit in the actual cash flow versus the planned cash flow. Provision must be made to cope with sudden unexpected expenses that may come up. Funds raised for a purpose must be utilised for that purpose only, as that provides a transparent picture of the organisation to lenders and investors, if any.

The entrepreneurial journey starts with investment. One of the reasons why people shy away from becoming an entrepreneur is because of the investments required to begin a business and the risks involved. However, if you have a great idea and you have done the four-point assessment (given below) to ratify its viability, if you love the idea and believe that you will leave no stone unturned in translating your idea into a great business plan, then you must go ahead full steam.

The four-point evaluation of your idea encompasses the following:

1. **Advice from experienced entrepreneurs and business forums:** Taking advice from proven experts will validate the idea and the market potential and let you create a sound business plan. Look at people who are able to evaluate your idea and add value without any prejudice. Most business ideas would not have seen the light of day if not for the correct advice sought at the outset. If your gut feeling is strong and there is market research feedback that it is worth the effort, go for it.

2. **Market research:** Do enough market research to understand the other options available in the market that are similar to your product/service. What is the target audience size for your product/service? Based on present-day conversion data, what is the business you can generate? Will the margins allow for business expansion? Try your best to get a comprehensive understanding of these and other, relevant factors.

3. **Business plan for funding:** Write down a business plan with the funding required for sustaining your venture. Put down everything you can think of, such as the cost of starting business, the working capital required, the amount of total funding required, and so on. Although it is best to have at least six months to a year's funding at your disposal, your business idea will have to show potential value to investors to attract them to invest in it.

4. **Method/source of funding:** Plan how you will get the finance to move ahead in your project. Who are the people who will fund your idea and when can they come on board? You can even have pre-set timelines for funding over a period, so that you can build value into your idea and acquire ready finance when needed.

Now let's look at the major sources of funding:

1. **Your own money:** Most entrepreneurs set aside some money of their own to finance their project. The advantage here is that since it is your money, you are not answerable to anyone on how you are using it. Moreover, there is always the satisfaction of doing something on your own. The downside is in case the business does not do well, you would incur personal loss, and you may also not be privy to free advice from experienced investors which comes in handy.

2. **Family and friends:** There are many entrepreneurs who are able to get money from family and friends. This is easy to get as it is based on goodwill and you have flexible payback options. The downside is, again, you do not bring any value to the table, you get only capital, since they do not understand the feasibility of your project.

3. **Crowd-funding:** Crowd-funding has become a really big phenomenon in today's world where you can seek funding from a large number of people. This platform is really picking up in the online space. There are many projects which have shaped up with this kind of funding. For example, Wishberry is a crowd-funding company for creative projects, such as making films, music videos, etc., which has helped people raise amounts ranging from ₹20 lakh to ₹10 crore.

4. **Angel investors:** Angels are wealthy individuals or retired corporate executives who are keen to invest as well as bring value to the venture in the form of knowledge. They are experts in their field and are keen to bring their domain knowledge into the business by helping to manage or supervise it. They look forward to a transparent system and, in technical terms, they want to be on the board of the company in exchange for putting up their money. To approach them, you

may need to look at specialised networking groups or angel website networks.

5. **Bank loans:** Bank loans are the most commonly used source of funding for small and medium-sized businesses. Consider the fact that all banks offer different advantages, whether it's personalised service or customised repayment. Hence, it is a good idea to shop around a bit at first and find a bank that meets your specific needs.

   In general, you should know that bankers look for companies that have a sound track record and excellent credit. A good idea is not enough; it has to be backed up with a solid business plan. Start-up loans would typically require a personal guarantee from the entrepreneurs. There is the start-up financing option for entrepreneurs in the start-up phase or the first 12 months of sales, where the principal repayment can be postponed for 12 months.

6. **Government grants and subsidies:** All governments work on supporting the start-up businesses. In India, there are over 50 schemes rolled out by the Indian government, including the Venture Capital Assistance Scheme, New Gen Innovation and Entrepreneurship Development Centre (NewGen IEDC), Performance & Credit Rating Scheme, Aspire—Scheme for Promotion of Innovation, Entrepreneurship and Agro Industry, among others. The main objective of such schemes is to give grants to support development of entrepreneurship, or to support entrepreneurs by providing funds through one-time as well as term loans.

   There are many bodies actively working in this space, including the Atal Innovation Mission, Niti Aayog, Department of Electronics and Information Technology, Software Technology Parks of India, Small Farmers Agri-Business Consortium,

CreditGuaranteeFund,andNationalSmallIndustriesCorporation who help to fund starts-ups, SMEs, MSMEs, and so on for limited amounts.

You can browse their website and see which of them will support your kind of business, based on which you can then approach them to pitch your idea.

It is vital to remember that the decision to go in for funding has to be made keeping in mind the long-term goals of the business as well as the ways and means of using the funding obtained to grow the wealth of stakeholders and investors, while adding value to the organisation.

13

Business Entities, Trademarks, Patents, and Other Legalities

When starting a new venture, one of the first legal considerations an entrepreneur needs to work on is the selection of the type of business entity. The Limited Liability Partnership Act and the Companies Act, 2013 allow choices of business entities. As an entrepreneur, you must take into account all the pros and cons of the various options available before choosing the one that will be right for you. It is a critical decision that will impact your individual liability, the amount of tax you pay, the paperwork you may need to maintain, as also your ability to raise money.

The options available in India are outlined below.

1. **Proprietorship:** In this kind of firm, the promoter's name can be used. No approvals are required, but one must refrain from using trademarked names. This type of company is not recognised as a separate legal entity, and the promoter/ proprietor is personally liable for all liabilities of the proprietorship. In India, foreigners are not allowed to start a proprietorship. Furthermore, the proprietorship can't be transferred and its existence is dependent on the proprietor. Taxes are calculated on the individual income of the proprietor.

2. **Partnership:** A partnership can either be registered or it can remain unregistered, as registration of this type of business entity is optional. If registered, a partnership is registered under the Partnership Act, 1932. As in the case of a proprietary business, the promoter's choice of name can be used for the partnership. No approval is necessary for using names; yet, it is best to avoid trademarked names. A partnership is not recognised as a separate legal entity, and the promoters

are personally liable for the liabilities of the partnership. A minimum of two persons are required to start a partnership. The maximum number of partners permissible is 20. Foreigners are not allowed to start a partnership. Also, a partnership is not transferable. Existence of a partnership business is dependent on the partners and it could be up for dissolution due to death of a partner. Partnership profits are taxed at 30 per cent plus surcharge and cess as applicable in India.

3. **Limited Liability Partnership (LLP):** An LLP is registered with the Ministry of Corporate Affairs under the Limited Liability Partnership Act, 2008. The choice of name provided by the promoter must be approved by the Registrar of Companies. Only names that are not identical/similar to that of any existing company, or LLP names that are not offensive or illegal, are allowed. The name of the entity must end with the words 'Limited Liability Partnership' or 'LLP'. An LLP is a separate legal entity registered under the Limited Liability Partnership Act, 2008. The partners in an LLP are not personally liable for the liabilities of the LLP. The partners have limited liability and are liable only to the extent of their contribution to the LLP. A minimum of two persons are required to start an LLP. Such an entity can have unlimited number of partners. Foreigners are allowed to invest in it only with prior approval of the Reserve Bank of India (RBI) and the Foreign Investment Promotion Board (FIPB). Ownership can be transferred. Existence of an LLP is not dependent on the partners and it can be dissolved only voluntarily or by an order of the Company Law Board. LLP profits are taxed at 30 per cent plus surcharge and cess as applicable. An LLP must file an annual statement of accounts and solvency and annual returns with the Registrar each year. Income Tax returns must also be filed for the LLP.

4. **One Person Company (OPC):** An OPC is registered with the Ministry of Corporate Affairs under the Companies Act, 2013. The choice of name provided by the promoter must be approved by the Registrar of Companies. Only names that are not identical/similar to that of any existing company, or LLP names that are not offensive or illegal are allowed. The name of the entity must end with the words 'OPC' or 'One Person Company'. An OPC is a separate legal entity registered under the Companies Act, 2013. The director and nominee director in such an entity are not personally liable for the liabilities of the company. The director and nominee director have limited liability and are liable only to the extent of their share capital. An OPC can have only two people, viz., director and nominee director. The director and nominee director cannot be foreigners. Ownership can be transferred. Existence of an OPC is not dependent on the director or nominee director. Such a firm can be dissolved only voluntarily or by regulatory authorities. An OPC's profits are taxed at 30 per cent plus surcharge and cess as applicable.

5. **Private Limited Company:** This type of firm is registered with the Ministry of Corporate Affairs under the Companies Act, 2013. The choice of name provided by the promoter must be approved by the Registrar of Companies. Only names that are not identical/similar to that of any existing company, or names that are not offensive or illegal are allowed. The name of the entity must end with the words 'Private Limited Company'. A private limited company is a separate legal entity registered under the Companies Act, 2013. The directors and shareholders of such a firm are not personally liable for the liabilities of the company. Shareholders have limited liability and are liable only to the extent of their share capital. A minimum of two persons are required to start a private limited company. Such a company can have a maximum of 200 shareholders or members.

Foreigners are allowed to invest in it under the Automatic Approval route in most sectors. Ownership can be transferred by way of share transfer. Existence of a private limited company is not dependent on the directors or shareholders. It can be dissolved only voluntarily or by regulatory authorities. A private limited company's profits are taxed at 30 per cent plus surcharge and cess as applicable. Board and general meetings must be conducted periodically. A private limited company must file annual accounts and annual returns with the Registrar of Companies. Income Tax returns must also be filed for the company.

Depending on the growth and business plan drawn up, you can choose the type of company you wish to register. However, you must keep in mind that this is an important decision which will impact your business in many important ways.

There are four things you must evaluate when finalising the kind of business entity you want to opt for. These are:

1. **Legal liability:** You need to gauge the kind of liability your business is prone to and give thought to whether you are, as an individual, willing to take responsibility for that liability. If not, then sole proprietorship and partnership businesses are not for you, because in the eventuality of facing a lawsuit, your own personal assets can also be at risk. However, if the benefits of a proprietary business in your case are greater, you could go in for an insurance policy to deal with such adverse situations.

2. **Taxation:** Another thing to consider is the minimum amount of tax you are likely to be required to pay, based on the nature of your individual business and its long-term goals. In the initial phase, when losses may be incurred, the personal taxation liability in proprietary and partnership businesses would be much lower.

3. **Incorporation cost and the paperwork required:** You must also factor in the amount of paperwork to be maintained as well as the costs incurred in setting up the business, when deciding which type of legal entity your business should choose.

4. **Flexibility and future needs:** While setting up an enterprise, it may be difficult to foresee long-term requirements, which is why it makes sense to evaluate options based on the individual nature of your business.

Thus, when starting any venture, there are numerous points you need to consider, beginning with registering the company, trademarks, and patents. A legal expert must be consulted to understand the licenses required for operating the business and setting up shop. Licenses will vary based on the business model. For example, in retail businesses, retail licenses would be required, practising licences for specialised staff, shop and establishment licenses, export and import licenses, and so on. Moreover, if you are entering into a lease agreement to rent out a place, do your homework meticulously and work towards taking a long lease, as the cost of readying infrastructure and interiors for the retail space used must be borne. Enter into legal agreements with vendors and business associates seeking the help of a legal team to avoid any problems that may crop up later.

Customer consent for specialised services should be taken to protect your brand from any uncalled for complaints. It is best to have a consultant lawyer at hand during the initial setting up of your business, in order to validate agreements and seek the requisite legal advice.

14

The Entrepreneurial Streak to Make It Happen

The essence of successful entrepreneurship lies in an attitude that keeps one relentlessly driven to create a business enterprise, tirelessly working to find solutions to the numerous hurdles that are faced in operating, marketing and garnering revenue for the entity. Meticulous planning and execution are the very backbone of success. However, there will always be that one aspect which is not in our control—the external environment—that will create hiccups, and it is at such times when one is tested, that one must not give up, rather keep moving. Remember, our mind is capable of finding alternative solutions to all kinds of problems, and we need to have a core team which can assist us in finding ways and means to solve them. Every individual has some or other specialised skills, so a partner or the members in a core team will bring their unique thought processes and skill sets to the table. Effective leadership entails evaluating the options and taking the best solution forward.

As an entrepreneur, it is important that you have a well delineated plan for the results that you want, and accordingly follow a process to achieve them. It is critical that the revenue/profits be defined with clarity in three business plans. Plan A could be the ideal blueprint on which your business is based. Plan B could be a forecast that aims slightly lower. And Plan C could outline the minimum revenue/profits you want to achieve. Be aware of the overall time frame, and the way in which you will need to run your business and cash flows based on the same. Understanding the goals of revenue and profitability will steer you towards them by understanding the other parts of your business plan and how those need to be tweaked to drive business.

A great product must be well known in the market, so marketing becomes a necessary part of any business. A new business must judiciously evaluate how low-cost marketing can build a strong customer base and credibility in the market space. Fortunately, with high use of digital and mobile marketing methods, there are many options available today that can help grow a business. However, consistency in the marketing plan is a must. Repeated marketing communication will attract customers who can then, through an effective loyalty programme and referral scheme, further drive your business by bringing in repeat purchase.

An entrepreneur can cultivate and enhance the performance of an organisation by working on the below parameters:

1. **Understanding your strengths and collaborating with people who can fill in the gaps:** Every individual has certain strengths unique to him/her. As an entrepreneur, you must focus on understanding your personal strengths and seeing how these can be used effectively to build your organisation. Seek to contribute in those areas. Without a doubt, you would need to be proficient in the financial and strategic aspects of the business. And if you aren't, then you must not hesitate to enrol in courses to acquire knowledge in those areas. Even if you partner with experts in those functions, you must have sufficient understanding to be able to add value as well as to question actions and decisions when required, so that people around you take your authority seriously and know that you can't be taken for a ride. Even if you let the mantle of things you are not an expert in rest in the hands of specialists, your knowledge and proficiency will allow you to build greater efficiencies in the organisation. Ultimately, work on building an organisation that excels in at least one field, so that it can build a niche for itself in that space. This can be done by identifying specific strengths and developing those diligently.

Organisations need to perform profitably, and that is possible only when there is overall efficiency across all aspects of the business. Yet, it is important to find the USP that, once honed, will bring you closer to the goals you wish to achieve.

For example, Byju's, the young educational giant in India, has followed the consultancy route to create a special place for itself. The staff they appointed were trained effectively and called a consultant. This consultant conducts a small test for the students and tries to assess the student's level by understanding the gaps in learning. Then they work on the perfect app that would provide the right solution to the student. They also build support via online knowledge gurus for weaker students. The brand clearly realised that education is about knowledge, and if they build a team of knowledgeable sales people, then making inroads in getting people to invest in an online programme that is priced on the higher side will become easier. Furthermore, by catching students young, they brought in a loyalty factor that would help build a wide student base for professional entrance test training courses.

2. **Effective management skills:** An entrepreneur must develop solid skills in time management and the capacity to plan and develop every part of the business, even though there may be a specialist team in place. The basic ability to draw up plans and look at time-bound outcomes will aid in spearheading a team appointed to achieve the desired results. Introspection and the ability to learn from others are two valuable assets when it comes to objectively and rationally evaluating set plans and leading the way forward. A day has a finite number of hours, and as an entrepreneur, you would need to prioritize work that falls in that quadrant which needs your constructive time and review. This is especially important in the initial period after you set up the business and when you are the visionary driving the goals of the organisation.

Strategic decision making must involve the management team, because sometimes you may miss out on some key points and someone else in the team may be able to provide a new perspective or enrich the decision-making process. Sam Walton attributes the success of Walmart to the method of delegating day-to-day operations to professionals, giving them maximum authority and responsibility, while he himself played a purely advisory role. The professional team built systems and invested in digitalising early on in the business cycle, making information flow easy, helping to build and monitor efficiencies in the business. Walton had limited knowledge in these aspects, and he was initially opposed to investing money in them. But he went ahead with his leadership team's decisions, thereby building collaborative productivity for the business.

3. **Communication skills and interpersonal skills:** As success in an endeavour is based on the ability to align people to a common goal and to build trust and clarity by communicating and forging relationships of trust, the ability of an entrepreneur to communicate clearly as well as to create a team that trusts him completely is essential for business success. Additionally, an entrepreneur engages with vendors, investors, and collaborative businesses, so he/she must possess a knack for infusing positive energies in these engagements to be able to get them to support his goal and business.

4. **Leadership skills:** Leadership is defined as the ability to influence people and pass on one's vision/plan/goal through one's passion and ability to communicate effectively, in such a way that they become aligned to your goals. However, as a good leader, you must understand that people will get aligned to a common goal only if there is something in it for them. If you keep thrusting your goals on them, they will not be oriented in letter and spirit to the common goal. Instead, if you try understanding their own personal goals and align

them to a common organisational goal, chances of building a team made up of the right people are much higher. Basketball champion Michael Jordan once said, "Talent wins games, but teamwork and intelligence wins championships." Hence, an entrepreneur must work on building a team that fully believes in his vision by intelligently utilising his leadership skills.

5. **Hands-on approach:** Success in any endeavour requires a hands-on approach. Entrepreneurs who, particularly in the formative years of their venture, delve deep into the business by interfacing with customers, team members, technical teams are able to build robust organisations, as they are able to both understand issues at the ground level and transfer their own passion for the business to the team members who then start emulating the commitment levels shown by the entrepreneur. This creates a culture of conducive growth.

The journey of being an entrepreneur can be very challenging yet extremely satisfying and enthralling provided the focus and discipline required to keep going is there. Almost every successful business story is centred on the infallible human tendency to passionately follow one's dream. There will be challenges and deterrents along the way, but the childlike resolve to keep going is what will be the driver to help one ultimately achieve success. It is quite like a child wanting to learn cycling. He will keep falling down and getting hurt, but every time that happens, he needs to get up, brush off the injury and continue cycling, until he learns how to cycle smoothly and effortlessly. Similarly, in every business journey too, there will naturally be hurdles and pitfalls, but the entrepreneur's resilience and resolve to keep going will definitely keep him/her on track.

I would like to quote the story of Mr Sridhar Vembu, CEO of Zoho Corp, an online application business. He was born in Chennai in a modest middle-class family. Both his parents had never been to college; his father served as stenographer in the high court. But Sridhar was destined for bigger things. He focussed on his education and went on to study electrical engineering at IIT Madras, following it up with a PhD from Princeton University. He started his career at Qualcomm Inc. as a wireless systems engineer, where he had the opportunity to work with leading minds in the field of wireless communication. Inspired, he co-founded Advent Net (an innovative online applications provider) in 1996, a software company serving network equipment vendors. He maintained growth and profitability without needing outside capital. He then set up Zoho, which competes successfully with the core products of Microsoft, Salesforce.com, and Google, that too without banking on any outside capital. Today, Zoho would be valued at well over $1 billion.

This kind of success has been possible only by sweating it out, staying focused on goals, and working with single-minded resolve towards those defined goals. If you have a dream and the resilience to go after it relentlessly, giving it your all, day after day... if you can work so hard as to turn the winds in your favour during trying times through sheer perseverance and strategic input, then you must go ahead and live the dream.

Entrepreneurship is a journey of following your aspirations,

Building it with passion and living up to it with inspiration,

It is not for the heart that is faint,

It is for the mind that is driven and resilient,

If you can get up every day to follow your dream,

Knock down every hurdle that dares to be seen,

Then you will in this entrepreneurial journey with exultation,

Create a world that will make you look back with gratification.

About the Author

Seema Singh Bhadoria has diverse experience in various industries in senior leadership roles in top notch multinational brands and Indian conglomerates spanning industries as diverse as telecom, multi-level marketing, real estate, media, and the wellness sector. She was the Chief Executive Officer of Richfeel Health and Beauty Pvt Ltd, where she served for seven years and was the driving force in making it the leader in its category. She had an outstanding track record of providing strategic direction and leading businesses towards achieving rapid growth and profitability by streamlining operations and creating a culture conducive to growth.